The Long Skip Home

Lisa Belknap

Veery Glade Publishing

The Long Skip Home

Scripture from the Holy Bible,
King James Version (KJV): public domain;
New International Version®, NIV®.
Copyright © 1973, 1978, 1984, 2011
By Biblica, Inc. TM.
Used by permission of Zondervan.
All rights reserved worldwide.

ISBN 978-1-7327930-2-6

Library of Congress Control Number: 2024917658

Veery Glade Publishing
Cortland, New York

For Matthew

He that hath ears to hear, let him hear.

Matthew 11:15

Chapters

Chapter One

I Will Follow

"Did you hear me?"

A hummingbird darted to and from the feeder hanging on the porch of Lily's family home in the woods. The quick bird sliced through the air in a swooping arc. Its chattering held Lily's attention better than her mother's question did. She faced her mother. "What?"

Sunlight poured behind her mother through the tops of maple trees to the grassy glade in front of their woodland home. Her mother picked at dirt stuck between her fingers while resting her arms on a small table. "I asked you how your piano playing went today."

Lily shrugged. She stared at a freshly planted red geranium. Was there any reason to tell her mother what happened at the seventh-grade chorus concert? Should she mention the crumpled piece of paper the size of a softball that, out of nowhere, landed on the piano keys and bounced between her hands while she accompanied the chorus? Should she mention how frantic she was, how she couldn't stop playing to remove it?

Lily forced a smile even though she knew she had been the butt of somebody's joke. "It went well."

And in the end, it had. Miss Nilsson, the chorus director, plucked the paper wad right off the piano keys during the performance. Lily didn't even make a mistake, thanks to months of practice.

Her mother smiled and waved a pesky fly from her face. "I'm glad. All your practicing has paid off. You're done with school, now. And, you can relax." She fanned her face with her hand. "It's hot! Why don't you go change? You'll feel better."

Lily agreed and picked up the backpack she had tossed next to the chair. She scuffed into the house.

Her mother called from the porch. "There's lemonade in the fridge. Would you bring us some?"

"Sure, Mom."

Lily dug through the dresser drawer for her favorite red tee shirt and pulled it down to her shorts. Cooler and feeling better, she left her bedroom and headed for the kitchen. She opened the refrigerator door, took out the pitcher of lemonade and poured the beverage into two glasses over plenty of ice.

Slipping on flip-flops by the door, she headed back to the porch and put the glasses on the table on the porch.

A delicate glass butterfly perched on a glass twig centered on the table caught the afternoon sunlight. Lily gently placed her hands on the edge of the table while she sat. Graceful blue wings stood open and two thin sticks of glass formed the antennae. "What's this?"

Her mother's eyes sparkled. "A blue morpho. I found it at a garage sale this morning before work."

"It's beautiful!"

"I agree. We'll have to go garage sale-ing this summer, you and I." Her mother sipped lemonade.

Lily loved garage sale-ing with her mom. They often found interesting things. She pulled off her ponytail holder and re-gathered her messy reddish-brown hair. "Mom, can I ask you something?"

"Sure."

Lily looked into her mother's blue eyes, the same blue as her eyes. "We're supposed to love our enemies, right?"

"Right."

Lily searched her mother's expression, wondering if there were exceptions to that rule. But when her mother didn't flinch, Lily sighed. "But Mom, how can anyone do *that*? I mean, that's what enemies do. They *hate* each other."

Her mother arched an eyebrow, conveying a usual wisdom. "Well, sometimes it's up to us to be the first to give a little."

Lily sank back into her chair and let her hand slap her thigh. *Give? Mom has no idea. How can I give anything to someone*

9

lousy, like the person who threw the wad when I was playing the piano? Lily stared at her mother.

Her mother took another sip of her lemonade. "I admit it's hard to do. God never said it would be easy."

"That's for sure." The ice settled in Lily's glass.

As long streaks of sunshine beamed through the maple trees, Lily knew her mother was right. Her mother's answer was based on the Bible, which Lily wanted to obey. But it was difficult sometimes, especially always being the new kid in school, having changed schools three times since the third grade, and encountering hard-to-love students.

Her mother put her glass down. "We must try to be gracious to others as Jesus is to us."

Lily nodded.

The front door swung open and Lily's older brother Josh stuck his head out. "Your phone's ringing, Mom." He jetted back into the house as their mother sprang up to answer it.

After a moment, Lily glugged down her lemonade, feeling the sugar rejuvenate her. She got up, leaned over the porch railing and studied a bluish-green hummingbird. As the bird balanced itself on a sprig of the yew bush in front of the porch, waiting for a turn at the feeder, Lily knew she didn't want to be in any situation where she would have to love an enemy.

Buzz!

A yellow jacket buzzed close to her face. Lily jerked her head back. "Get away!" She swung at the bee but missed. The bee swooped around and advanced her. She backed up and swatted again. Missed. Then, she backed up again and bumped into the table behind her. Quickly, she turned around and reached for the lemonade glasses before they fell over. But she could do nothing to prevent the glass butterfly from tipping over. A wing and both antennae broke off.

"No!" Lily swung again and hit the yellow jacket to the floor. She stomped on the bug and smeared it. She turned to the broken butterfly and huffed. *Great.* She pulled the chair in and sat. *Why me?* She picked up the broken wing and fit the pieces together. *Maybe I can glue it back together again.* But when her mother returned, Lily quickly hid the sharp pieces in her hands.

"That was your father on the phone. He's picking up a pizza after work." Her mother sat down then frowned at Lily's closed hands.

Lily looked at her mother and then her hands and then back at her mother as she slowly opened them. The broken glass pieces fell on the table. Her heart sank at the sad look on her mother's face. "I'm … I'm sorry, Mom. But I'm sure I can fix it!"

Lily ran into the house, found the super glue in the buffet, brought it back to the table, applied the glue, held it for a minute, and then let go. It stuck. She smiled at her mom.

Her mother returned the smile but then looked perplexed. "But what happened?"

Lily snarled her lip at the smooshed bee. "That stupid bee was trying to sting me! He kept coming after me. But I swung at him. And then I bumped into the table. I didn't mean it."

Her mother sighed then took Lily's hands in hers. "Oh, of course you didn't mean it. I know that. And the bees do get bad around here. I'm glad you didn't get stung." She inspected

11

her daughter's hands, rubbing her thumbs gently over Lily's palms. "Or cut. I wouldn't want these talented hands to be injured. It looks like the glue is holding. It's just a knick-knack. Don't worry about it." Her mother squeezed her hands and then let go. She carefully picked up the butterfly. "I'll place this in a safe place." She walked into the house.

Mom always had a way of staying positive, which wasn't always true with Lily and this day had become more discouraging than she could bear. She looked across the front yard to the woods on the other side of the road. Shadows from passing clouds crept across lush green leaves and then dissipated when the sun shone again.

Lily stepped off the porch and traipsed across the front yard. When she got to the road, she picked up a stone and threw it as hard as she could into the weeds. Maybe it would hit the kid who threw the wad. Or maybe ricochet back and hit her in the head for breaking the glass butterfly.

She moped across the street and trudged through the underbrush in the woods, not caring where she stepped until a thorny briar cut into her bare leg. "Ow!" She stopped to examine the wound. *Just a scratch.* She sighed, glanced back at home, then moved more carefully around other briars.

She set her sights on a secret place not visited often— except if you were a bird or a coyote, or you happened to be Lily Lightfoot.

When she reached the row of hemlock trees and could no longer see her home, she sighed. Her parents didn't like her wandering alone this far from home even though they trekked here a few times—she, her parents and two brothers, Henry and Josh. Josh didn't go as often anymore, though.

Lily stopped and peered up through the evergreen branches swaying in the breeze. "I'm no good, and I can't love enemies."

She waited for her voice to reach God in Heaven as she peered through hemlock boughs at a section of blue sky. When only a gentle breeze touched her arms and the mystical, spiraling tune of a veery thrush filled the woods, she looked down and kicked the tiny pinecones on the ground that had fallen from the evergreens. "But I know I'm supposed to."

The veery thrush encouraged her escape. There was no use in searching for the small brown deep-forested bird, being so elusive. Lily balanced herself across a log, listening to a woodpecker tap high above in the canopy of the woodland realm.

Soon, she arrived at the waterfall. Gushing water resonated in her ears. Water poured off a rocky ravine and echoed through the gorge. Cool overspray sprinkled her hot face, arms, and legs. The water ripped through carved-out rock and cascaded down a thirty-foot stone staircase just inches from her feet.

The waterfall was her second secret place in the woods, often stopped at before her favorite secret place.

At the base of a tree, Lily plopped herself down on a patch of moss with her shoulders slumped forward and her hands quiet on her lap. She rested her head against the tree trunk and breathed softly, letting the water drown out discouragement from school and even from the world, for there were many problems she had heard of, and of how difficult it was, sometimes, to be a Christian. *How can I love enemies, God? I don't really want to.*

Lily stood and then chose her steps carefully along a coyote path to a rock that jutted into the rapidly flowing brook further up from the waterfall. This was Peaceful Rock, her favorite secret place. Careful not to slip, she stepped onto the rock and sat on a dry spot as water trilled between rocks. A crayfish stared at her from under the water.

If I were a crayfish, I wouldn't have to deal with anything.

Lily huffed. She knew this was futile thinking. God didn't make her with a crustacean body, able to breathe under water. She was supposed to be in the world but not of it.

With the sounds of the babbling brook, spiraling songs of deep-woodland birds, and leaves rustling in the wind, Lily peacefully whispered memorized verses from a poem.

I will sit for many hours there,
or at least what seems to be,
and I'll hear the water sing His care,
of the love He has for me.

And my troubles will go down the way,
where the ravens tend to flock,
yet the perfect peace of God will stay,
trusting well on Peaceful Rock.

She prayed. "Dear Lord, thank you for helping me play the piano today even though I don't know who threw that paper

14

wad. But *You* do. I'm not good at loving enemies so help me do that. Also, please help me to not be discouraged, and that the glue would stick on mom's butterfly. In Jesus' name, Amen."

When Lily lifted her head, the sweet smell of roses wafted in and mingled with the rich earthy smells of the woodland. Lily drew in a deep sniff and closed her eyes. Then she scrunched her eyebrows and re-opened her eyes. *Wait a minute. That's odd. Roses?*

Snap!

Lily turned her head in the direction of the sharp sound. A flash of white streaked behind a group of dark green ferns. Something was in the woods with her. Lily scanned the undergrowth where the flash of white had been. Only a large green fern at the base of a tree flapped in the breeze.

Snap! Another stick broke. The white object darted behind another fern. *There it is again!*

Lily's heart raced as she pressed her fingers hard into Peaceful Rock, ready to spring to her feet. She moved her eyes from side to side and felt air pressing in on her bare skin.

Then, as if someone clicked the mute button on a remote control, the woods silenced. The birds stopped singing, the woodpeckers stopped tapping, the leaves stopped rustling, and amazingly, the sounds of babbling water faded away.

Lily's heart didn't stop pounding, though. She held her breath as a white animal approached. Lily stood quickly and planted her feet firmly on Peaceful Rock. She didn't want to call out to give away her location as the animal drew close.

A low fern folded back and out stepped a small white lamb.

The lamb's white fleece glowed against dark green ferns in an uncommonly way. Two large ears flicked when he let out a bleat. Dark brown eyes met Lily's. The lamb shifted his weight on small hooves and fluffy frill filled his fleecy face.

Lily let out a relieved, shaky laugh. "Where did you come from?" She stepped forward but the lamb bolted back into the woods. "Wait! I'm not going to hurt you!"

Lily chased the lamb, ducking under branches and zigzagging around tree trunks. She grabbed saplings and pulled herself up a slope, trying to keep up with the agile lamb having the advantage of four hooves over her worn-out flip flops. Fast as she ran, she couldn't catch the lamb.

She reached level ground and stumbled onto a path, grasping her knees and breathing heavy in and out. She stood and looked at a strange section of woods.

Where am I?

Lily blinked at two odd, narrow white stones marking each side of the path. She approached one and squinted at a design of a circle with two triangles affixed at the sides and nine straight lines shooting out around the design, like the rays of the sun.

A chilly gust of wind cut through the summer heat like a knife. Her ponytail whipped around her neck as she turned into the cold wind.

In a field of tall, swaying grass, the white lamb jumped up and down. "Baa!"

Lily stiffened, moving only her eyes from left to right. She had never seen a field there before. And was the only sound the whistling wind coming off the field?

The lamb turned, disappearing then reappearing in the grass as he gamboled away until he was out of sight.

Where did he go?

Lily took a step between the stone markers, and the muggy heat of summer blew away from chilly, mountainous air.

Chapter Two

And Be Welcomed

Lily looked back over her shoulder at the familiar shape of hemlock trees on the far side of the white marker stones. Home was not far and she could be there if she ran now. Plaintive bleating made her turn around. She rubbed her arms, tucked her head, and forged her way through cold air, determined to follow the lamb jumping through the grass. When Lily reached him at the edge of the field, she gaped.

This is impossible.

From a high mountain precipice, a large lake dominated the center of an immense valley. Lily's heart raced as she took in the scene of a rocky island covered with evergreen trees situated to the center right of the lake. She never recalled a lake being here. To the right of the lake, alternating green and brown fields stretched around and beyond a village, as far as her eye could see. On the other end of the lake, a city caught the rays of the afternoon sun. Lily shielded her eyes with her hand. A haze stretched beyond snow-covered mountains on the horizon. Over far distant jagged peaks, a dark sky hung like a black curtain.

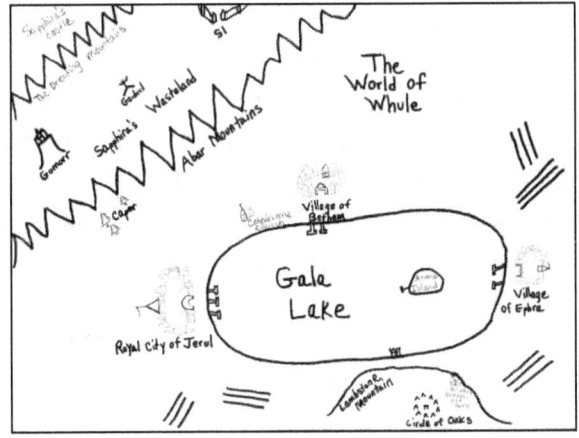

Where am I?

The lamb nudged Lily's leg, turned, and gamboled to the only feature on the field—a circle of trees several hundred feet away.

Alone on the precipice, Lily shivered in the gnawing wind as cold mountain air whipped around her bare arms and legs.

Am I alone?

19

Lily looked up at the sky. This strange place was not void of God. She knew in her heart that God was everywhere, and indeed in her heart, ever since she knelt beside her mother and asked Jesus in. She wasn't afraid—not much anyway—because she knew God loved her. He knew every hair on her head, even here, in this strange, new place.

No. I'm not alone.

She took another deep breath and exhaled. Her chest fluttered. She faced the side of a mountain wall. *Now that's odd. Why is there snow packed in the rock crevices but the grass is summertime green?* She turned to the circle of trees, searching for the lamb, wishing she had boots and warmer clothes.

Approaching the trees, Lily counted nine majestic oaks. Huge birds perched on each treetop. When she came closer, one bird screeched and soared into the sky—an eagle, five times bigger than normal! Lily crouched to the ground when the massive bird flew over her. She ducked when wind from its enormous wings flattened the grass around her. The other eagles soared off their treetops, and then the cliff, whistling high-pitched calls to each other.

"Baa!"

Lily spun around. "There you are!" The lamb stood at the base of one of the nine majestic oaks.

When she stepped into the circle of trees, the wind stopped. In the still, quiet air, she tried to be as quiet as a mouse as she surveyed a table of white stone in the center like an altar in a church. As she walked forward, she tipped her head back and traced intricate branches laced together that formed a green canopy. Something lumpy pierced through her flip flop. She moved her foot and saw an acorn, one of many speckling the ground covered with short grass.

Lily approached the altar table. Carvings of vines and leaves detailed the edges of the table. White roses, like at a wedding, wrapped around thick leg columns. She smelled one and the fragrance formed a lightness in her mind and warmth in her body.

On the tabletop, nine trees encircled a carving of a lamb. In each corner of the tabletop were carvings of a circle with two triangles on each side, the same as on the stone markers. Nine colored gems—red, yellow, blue, brown, pink, purple, green, orange, and indigo—sparkled in an arch at the back of the tabletop. Beneath them, words were engraved in a language Lily didn't recognize.

"Baa."

Lily knelt to touch the lamb for the first time, burying her fingers in fine fleece fibers softer than she imagined. She savored the warmth from his body. Holding his head in her hands, she peered into his warm brown eyes. "Your pupils are rectangular!"

He flicked his ears then touched his pink nose to hers.

She giggled. "I have to admit, this is kind of strange."

"Baa." He nodded his head, then turned and trotted out of the circle of oaks.

"Now where are you going?"

Lily stood and then froze. Strolling through the grass, a woman dressed in a white gown approached the trees. Lily's eyes flashed back and forth. *Where can I hide?* She quickly crouched behind one of the back legs of the table and pressed

21

her head hard into the leg, hoping to blend in. Chit-chat calls and the sound of flapping wings burst in the canopy above her. She gripped the table leg when the large eagles returned to their places, their talons grabbing tree limbs to land.

The woman entered the circle of oaks. "Hello!" she called in a sing-song voice. "Please stand up and tell me who you are."

Lily wished she could dig an escape tunnel back to home.

After a moment, the woman spoke again. "Please, don't be afraid. I will not hurt you. You must be of extreme importance for the eagles to have flown."

Lily's heartbeat pounded in her ears. She didn't move. What could she do next? She felt trapped until something brushed the side of her hair. She jerked her head, thinking it was the woman. But it was something smaller. A blue morpho butterfly fluttered close to her ear. It flapped its large delicate wings, hovering in place. *What a beautiful butterfly!*

The woman leaned over the table and met Lily's eyes. "I said 'hello'," her voice sang.

Lily locked eyes with the woman. Her face seemed too young for the white hair hanging in long soft waves. A collar of white lace adorned her white dress. Butterflies fluttered above her head and along her long, belled sleeves.

The woman extended a hand but Lily didn't take it. She grasped the edge of the table instead as she stood, glancing over to the stone markers, gauging the distance to them. If she had to, she could make a mad dash for them.

The woman took a step back. "I am Briella the White. Who are you and where did you come from?"

Lily missed the question. She was too busy watching butterflies land on the woman's head while others perched on her shoulders and down her sleeves to her wrists. The blue morpho butterfly that brushed her hair landed on Briella's hairline above her forehead, seeming to be the most important butterfly. And around her waist, a purple sash held a bouquet of red and purple flowers tucked in a pouch.

"I repeat, who are you and where did you come from?" Briella's voice, still kind, had grown firm.

Lily's stomach tightened. She focused. "I … I'm Lily Lightfoot. I came from over there." She pointed to the stones at the edge of the woods.

Swoosh! A quick wind brushed by Lily and made her shudder. *What just happened?* Briella was no longer in front of her. Lily looked at the stones and Briella had swooshed to them!

How did she get over there so fast?

Lily searched the ground for a moving escalator or wires or a fast-moving cart. She didn't see anything. When Briella flew back, she snapped her head back. As Briella's white hair settled, white butterflies landed on her head while colorful ones fluttered again to her belled sleeves.

"And what *caused* you to come through those stones, you who has short ears?"

Lily looked at Briella's ears. They were no different than hers.

Briella peered left and right at Lily as if looking through a dirty window of an abandoned storefront. "Hello? Are you there, young lady?"

23

Lily pasted a fake smile on her face. She studied Briella's peculiar outfit. "Are … are you going to a costume party?"

Briella stretched her neck higher. "No."

Lily's perplexed look fell on the woman's pouch of flowers. "Are you with … with the circus?"

Briella squared her shoulders and then laughed. "Circus? Of course not!"

Lily swallowed, trying to place the woman's type of gown with the correct time period. "Is there a medieval play around here?"

"No! Now, Miss Lightfoot, you answer *my* question. I asked you what made you come through those stones. You have not answered me." The white butterflies on Briella's head held their wings open while the blue morpho in the front flapped its wings rapidly.

Lily bit her lip. Was there enough distance between her and this strange woman? Was this woman as good a runner as she was? Lily looked down at her flip flops, a serious disadvantage, then back at Briella, repeating the question. "What made me come *through* the stones?"

Briella nodded.

"I followed a lamb."

Briella pinned Lily with an intense stare. "A lamb?"

A nervous feeling knotted in Lily's stomach. She drew out her reply. "Ye-es."

Briella's face grew brighter and her white gown glowed. The blue morpho butterfly flew in front of her, its head facing hers before zipping over to the altar table. Briella hurried around and pointed to the carving of the lamb on the table.

24

"The lamb you saw, does it look like this?"

Lily nodded, wondering what else a lamb would look like.

Briella faced the altar, dropped to her knees, bowed her head, and closed her eyes while her butterflies closed their wings and held their positions, even the blue morpho.

Keeping her eyes on Briella, Lily took a step backward, glancing at the markers. This might be the time to run.

Briella stood and faced Lily. "Miss Lily Lightfoot, I, Briella the White, bid you a most sincere welcome to this, our world of Whule, where long we have awaited the appearance of the lamb. I see you are cold. My cottage is not far." She pointed across the field. "You'll be warm there."

Lily stumbled backward, placing a hand on the rough surface of a tree trunk. "Uh, no thank you. I should probably go home now."

Briella held a hand out. "I'm not sure how to convince you. Lily, you can trust me. Because you followed the lamb here, no harm will befall you."

Lily's mind scrambled. She held her stance, ready to push off the trunk as her words stumbled out. "My family will wonder where I am."

Briella looked down and readjusted her sash. "No, they will not."

Lily's mind raced. Worry set in her stiff stance. She wrinkled her brow as her heart pounded.

Briella spoke calmly. "Calm down. What if I told you that you will return to your world at the exact time you left it? No one will even miss you."

Lily didn't budge.

25

"Did you hear me?" Briella put her face in front of Lily's, her eyes blue depths of mystery. "I said your family will not miss you. You won't even miss dinner!" Briella smiled.

"Pfft! That's hard to believe."

"Well, it's true!"

Briella's quick reply left little room for Lily to doubt her. Still, she murmured, "How do you know?"

Briella swung her arms out. "Because I am Briella the White and I can do things others can't."

Lily smirked.

Briella flicked her pointer finger. "I see you require proof. Observe."

Briella jumped high to the tops of the oak trees and twirled around several times. White doves flew from her. She lifted her arms and the birds flew around the inside of the circle and then past the oak trees and into the wind. When she returned to the ground, her butterflies resettled on her head, shoulders, and sleeves.

Lily staggered against the tree. Goose bumps spread across her arms and down her back. "Are … are you an angel?"

An upward curve in Briella's smile hinted at vast knowledge. "I have been likened to one. Know that you can trust me. I will protect you. I know with one hundred percent certainty that you will return safely to your home. Coming?"

One hundred percent certainty? Thoughts whisked around in Lily's mind like babbling brook water around Peaceful Rock. She could count on the peace of home and the love of her parents. They would be there when she got back. But can a stranger be trusted?

26

"Well, will you come with me?"

Lily scratched her fingers into the grooves of the tree bark behind her. *Am I getting an invitation from an angel? Does she work for God? Did she say no harm would befall me and that I'm of extreme importance? There is a Bible verse about being kind to strangers.* Lily managed a small nod.

Briella stepped forward and put her hands on Lily's shoulders. "I am most glad. You are a welcomed joy!" She checked her pouch and waved her hand in the air to disperse frilly butterflies. "Now, let's get you warmed up."

Lily looked for the lamb as they left the circle of trees but he was nowhere to be found. The blue morpho darted around her, helping distract her from the stinging cold on her bare arms, legs, and toes, which stuck out from her flip-flops.

"It's cold up here on Lambstone Mountain. You are hardly dressed for it. But my cottage is toasty. It's right at the end of this path." Briella's white gown flowed in the wind. She didn't shiver, making Lily wonder if she was even cold.

Red shutters flanked the windows of Briella's stone cottage and a white horse by a barn whinnied a welcome.

Briella opened the front door. "Here we are!"

Lily entered, wiped her feet, and breathed in a cinnamon aroma. Old pictures, mostly of birds, decorated the walls. She followed Briella into the kitchen where pots hung from a trellis-like rack above a table. A black kettle hung over a fire. A bird with a purple hat cooed on a stand by the window. Lily took a closer look. The purple hat matched the purple in his green and purple neck.

Briella sat at a desk. "That's Pity-Petty. He's the royal carrier pigeon." She took a feather pen, dipped it in ink, and wrote on a small piece of paper. "The king and queen of the royal city of Jerul will want to know about the lamb's appearance." Briella folded the note tightly and placed it in a small satchel. She strolled over to Pity-Petty, fit it across his chest, kissed him, and then opened the window.

"Make haste, Pity-Petty! You carry the most important message of your life!"

Pity-Petty hopped to the window sill. Before he jumped out, he turned his head and winked at Lily.

"Did you see that? I think he winked at me."

"He most likely did," said Briella.

The royal carrier pigeon spread his wings and tossed his body into the turbulent mountain air. His flight pattern swooped as he flew along the face of Lambstone Mountain. His shape grew smaller and smaller as he flew toward the dark horizon until he was gone.

"There goes Pity-Petty." Briella stared quietly after him and then slowly closed the window. "Come, have a seat at the table. Let's have something to eat."

Sensing sadness in Briella, Lily lifted a chair out from the table so it wouldn't scrape on the floor.

Briella picked up a flute that lay across the table. She moved it to the desk without a single butterfly falling off. Her upbeat mood returned. "Yes, I was playing the flute when I looked out the window and saw the eagles fly. Right at the end of my favorite song, they caught my eye and I said to Pity-Petty, 'I need to go check that out!'"

Lily was glad Briella was happy again, and that she was a musician.

Briella took bread out of the oven, placed it on a breadboard with a knife, and filled two bowls with stew from the kettle. "You see, I have waited a long time for the eagles to fly. Would you like honey or sugar in your tea?"

"Sugar, please. Thank you."

Briella handed Lily a small bowl of sugar and she added some to her tea. "Will Pity-Petty be okay?"

"Yes. He is a very capable flier. Thank you for asking about him."

The blue morpho perched above Briella's forehead. Lily moved to change her angle of view and the morpho's shiny blue wings changed to shimmering purple. "I think the wing color just changed."

"No, it did not. Bluey's dazzling iridescent wings appear blue, but not because of pigment. He has some very fancy scales on his wings that reflect light."

"Bluey?"

"Yes. He is a very special butterfly."

"He certainly has beautiful wings."

Bluey flapped his wings in between two large white morpho butterflies similar to him. Lily wondered what their names were but didn't ask. Two other white butterflies and two smaller ones in the back with long tails rested on Briella's head like a tiara. Red butterflies flapped their wings slowly on each shoulder. Yellow, blue and other butterflies flapped their wings slowly from her shoulders to her wrists.

Briella stirred honey into her tea. "I am not the only one who has waited for the flight of the eagles. Help yourself to some cinnamon bread and butter."

Lily spread a thin layer of soft butter on a piece of bread and took a bite, savoring the flavor.

"John, on the island of Atmos, has been waiting a long time—not as long as me, but still, a long time. We will restore here briefly and then go see him this very evening. He will be most glad to meet you."

Lily returned a smile by the biggest smile she had yet seen on this peculiar, white-haired, butterfly angel.

Chapter Three

Across the Water

Clutching the limbs of a dead tree, the vulture shifted his weight with the soft rustle of dark feathers. Pale eyes gleamed beneath ugly lumps on his scabby head. A disturbance on Lambstone Mountain caught his eye. He spread his wings and leaped from the lifeless, twisted perch, finding an updraft to carry him closer to the precipice. As he approached the circle of trees, his heart beat faster. The thing that had never happened in all his long years of watching had finally happened. The eagles had flown! With a piercing cry, he beat air currents with powerful wing strokes toward the distant dark sky to report to his master.

***

The path back to home lay inches from Lily's feet. She twirled the fringed end of a red scarf Briella lent her around her finger. The other end dangled to her hip. "Are you sure my family won't miss me?"

Briella steadied the horse and buggy. "Trust me. They will not. As I said, you will return at the exact moment you left. And I can ensure your safety one hundred percent."

Briella placed a hand on Lily's arm and peace radiated through the wool coat she now wore. As she took a deep breath, tension in her shoulders melted. *I'm pretty sure this angel is trustworthy. Who wouldn't trust their own angel?* Lily let her breath out and gave Briella a grin.

Briella looked Lily over. "The wool coat will serve you well."

Lily buttoned the coat. "Thank you." She bent over to tuck pant legs into leather boots. "And for the pants and boots too."

"You're welcome. By the time we get down Lambstone Mountain, you won't need them, but I advise we take them, nonetheless." Briella steadied the horse. "You are here in Whule for a reason."

"Do you know what that reason is?"

"That, I cannot answer. Even so, the journey is set before you." Briella motioned for Lily to get into the buggy.

Lily climbed in but stopped to look at Briella. "When you say you can't answer, do you mean you're not allowed to or you don't know the answer?"

"It is because I do not fully know."

Lily gave a slow nod then slid across the bench, making room for Briella who boosted herself up. *What did Briella mean that I am of great importance?* Lily did not think it proper to ask, however, as it might come off sounding arrogant. She didn't think she was of great importance. Still, she'd like to know the answer.

Grabbing the reins, Briella made a clicking sound with her tongue. "Walk on." They pulled away from the cottage on a road dusted with snow. "What I *do* know is there is a prophecy, and not too many remember it. The few who do are called a 'remnant.'" Briella arched an eyebrow at Lily. "There is always a remnant."

Remnant? What does that mean?

But before she could ask, Briella spoke again. "And they will be exceedingly glad to hear of the lamb's appearance."

Bluey and six white butterflies clung to strands of Briella's white hair as she steered the buggy down the mountain. Red, yellow, and blue butterflies flitted on her sleeves, and the rest rode on the white horse. The clip-clop of the horse's hooves echoed off pine trees along the frozen road. The late afternoon sun cast shadows between thick evergreen trees as they made their way down Lambstone Mountain.

"Yes, I was there in my kitchen playing "The Flight of the Butterfly" when I looked out the window and saw the eagles soaring high in the sky. Clear as day, they were flying!"

"Is that anything like "The Flight of the Bumblebee"?"

Briella shrugged. "I don't know. How does that go?"

"Really fast. It's supposed to sound like a bumblebee flying up and down and all around."

Briella shook her head. "No. That doesn't sound anything like "The Flight of the Butterfly". This piece should be played whimsically, like a fluttering flier flitting from flower to flower."

Lily giggled. "I'd like to hear that."

"I would be happy to play it for you sometime. I've been practicing for years. It's in a relatively easy key."

"Oh? What key is that?", curious if she really knew.

"E major. I take it you are a musician."

Wow. She knew. "Yes, I play the piano."

"Hmm. The piano? What's that?"

"The piano? You don't know what a piano is?" Lily's reply came out a tad snootier than she wanted.

Briella stared at Lily then back to driving the buggy and drew out her reply. "Nooo."

Lily's face grew warm. Had she offended the angel? She looked down. In all the places she had lived with her family, there was always a piano. "I'm sorry. I thought everyone knew what a piano is."

"That's all right," said Briella. "Tell me how you play it."

Briella's kind tone and gracious attitude lifted Lily's spirit. She brightened. "I sit on a bench and face a row of black and white keys before me, like at your desk. The keys move hammers inside the desk, or should I say 'cabinet'. It's like a piece of furniture, you see. And the hammers strike strings that vibrate and produce tones."

"Interesting. Have you played anything in the key of E?"

"The E major scale and arpeggio," said Lily. "And a sonata." Lily frowned. "So there aren't any pianos in Whule?"

Briella shook her head. "Not a one."

Lily slouched. "How can anyone live in a world without a piano?"

"I do. Many do. But maybe someday, this piano with keys, hammers, and strings will be built. Then you and I could play a flute and piano duet together. Would you like that?"

"Yes."

Briella chuckled. "As would I."

As they traveled down Lambstone Mountain, pine forests gave way to the green pastures of foothills. They passed tidy fields with straight lines left by a plow. With every mile, they drew closer to the lake until it dominated the landscape under a red-streaked evening sky. Small boats tied up at a dock rocked gently on the water's surface. A man fished from a railing while an older man wearing a captain's hat swept the dock.

Briella parked the buggy. "Brace yourself," she said under her breath, "Captain Grouse is a real rip." She hopped out. "Actually, so is Finn." She turned from the buggy and her voice rang out, "Good evening, Finn!"

Lily followed Briella to the dock and then stopped dead in her tracks. She stared at Finn fishing from the railing as her mouth dropped open. His large ears protruded out horizontally from the sides of his head and ended with a point! His messy brown hair covered his head with bangs sweeping his forehead. But no hair could possibly conceal the overgrown lamblike ears. Lily thought they were a costume.

Finn glanced at her then returned to fishing.

The pungent smell of body odor stung Lily's nostrils when she passed by him to catch up with Briella. His ratty

35

appearance was like a homeless man. Beads of water, whether from spray from the lake or sweat, left trails through grime caked on his face, and his messy hair looked like a rat's nest.

"And good evening to you, Captain Grouse."

"Yeah, evening," grunted Captain Grouse coming up to Briella. His ears stuck out too, about three inches, and supported a captain's hat. He didn't seem to have much hair.

Lily pointed. "Are those your *real* ears?"

Captain Grouse drew near to Lily. His hazel eyes pierced her with suspicion. "Yeah, they're my real ears." His onion breath almost knocked her out of her boots. "You got a problem with them?"

Lily shook her head quickly and held her breath. And although, regrettably and not meaning to (because who wouldn't be stunned by such ears), she had offended the captain, and also shocked herself into realizing this was not Earth. (Of course, seeing Briella had also contributed to that.)

Briella stepped in. "Captain Grouse, the evening light still shines on Gala Lake. Can you please take us out to Atmos Island?"

The captain rested his broom against the shed. Briella's butterflies flew in a flurry around his face.

"Hold your horses! And get these butterflies out of my face!" He swung at them but missed every one.

Lily smirked.

Captain Grouse peered at Lily again and she removed the smirk. "I've never seen anyone with *short* ears except Briella. Who is this, Briella? Is this your protégé—your apprentice in training?"

36

"She is my friend. Now, will you take us out to the island? You *do* make trips until dusk."

The captain rubbed his stubbly chin. "Yeah, but it's gettin' kinda late. It'll be dusk by the time Finn and I get back. Gonna have to charge you extra." He held out a hand for payment. "And up front."

"What?" Briella's voice raised and her butterflies fluttered rapidly again in front of the captain's face before swooping away.

Captain Grouse looked across the water. "It looks like dusk to me. Been a busy day. Don't even get me started! I was just closing up." He looked at Briella and pointed to the palm of his hand.

Briella huffed. "This is highway robbery! I will pay when service is rendered, like always. Now, let's get going. Which boat do we get in?"

The captain snapped at Finn. "Finn! Put that fishing pole down and get *Salty* ready!"

Finn ambled down the dock. Lily stepped aside to make sure he and his floppy ears had enough room to get by so he wouldn't touch her. He untied ropes to a rowboat.

"After you, ladies." Captain Grouse gestured.

"Come on, Lily," said Briella, getting into the rowboat.

Lily steadied herself as she made her way to the front seat. When the captain jerked an impatient thumb for her to sit down, she scrambled, not wanting to hold up progress, especially since he'd already had a bad day. Briella sat at the opposite end, her butterflies alighting once more on her head and sleeves.

The grouchy long-eared captain sat down on the middle bench with his back to Lily and took one of the oars. Finn pushed off, his long ears flicking from the movement, and joined the captain with the other oar. They pulled back their oars together in a smooth rhythm, the squeaky sound in their holders carrying across the water.

The last of the sun's rays reflected on the water and flashed in Lily's eyes.

Where is God taking me? Is this wise to be out on this lake? With strangers? With weird strangers with long ears?

Lily was afraid, but not much. Most of that fear flew away when Briella spoke.

The captain turned around. "You sure look like her protégé." He pointed to Lily's head. "You even got a butterfly on your head."

Lily looked up but, of course, she couldn't see the top of her head. She noticed Bluey wasn't in his usual place above Briella's forehead so she knew it was him. She held her head still, trying to provide a steady place for Bluey as the men rowed into the lake.

Finn asked while rowing, "Where are you from?"

Lily hesitated. How could she explain where she was from?

"Hello? You alive back there?"

Lily scrunched her nose as if smelling rotten eggs. "Yes."

"Well, why don't you say something?"

"I'm from Truxton."

"Oh yeah? Where's that?"

38

She could say what her father said when describing their small town's location. "It's about twenty miles south of Syracuse."

"Syracuse? Where's that?"

"In New York."

Finn looked at the captain. "Have you heard of these places?"

The captain shook his head.

Finn turned around. "What country are you from?"

Lily met Finn's brown eyes and whispered, "The United States."

Finn turned back around. "Never heard of it."

A sick feeling churned in Lily's stomach. *Why am I here? Where is Whule? And maybe I should have gone home.*

Bluey fluttered in front of Lily. His delicate blue morpho wings caught the last of the evening's light, and when his insect head bobbed up and down while his body curled left and right, Lily smiled.

"Be at ease, Lily," said Briella as Bluey flew back to her. "Everything will be fine."

Briella's voice produced a strange calmness like a cozy shawl around Lily's shoulders so that she could somehow endure Finn and Captain Grouse.

"Huh," huffed Finn, pulling back on the oar. "That's not what my buddy Dan says. He says the end time is here for sure."

The captain whined to Finn. "You can't believe anything that nincompoop says."

Briella raised her hand. "This time, he's right. Today, the eagles flew!"

Finn stopped rowing, forcing the captain to stop too. He rested his arm on the oar while the captain let out a long sigh, upset at the break in rowing. "The eagles flew?" Finn repeated with sarcastic emphasis.

Captain Grouse patted Finn's shoulder. "Easy, Finn. You know Briella. She's got cockeymania ideas. Come on, let's get our backs into this. I want to go home already." The captain nudged his shipmate to continue rowing.

Lily gripped the bench as the rowboat jerked forward.

"It's cockamamie…," mumbled Finn before raising his voice to Briella, "…as cockamamie as those ridiculous butterflies. Don't they bother you always sitting up there on the top of your head?"

Briella's face grew stern but she maintained her composure as the men continued rowing across Gala Lake.

"You know what I'd do?" Finn spoke as he pulled on the oar. "I'd swat them, every last one. I'd scoop up their miserable tiny remains and sprinkle them into fertilizer for my uncle's garden."

The captain snickered. "Maybe his tomatoes would taste better!"

"I doubt it." Finn snapped back at Briella. "Don't you worry what people say? They say you're a nut—a crazy woman who lives alone on Lambstone Mountain waiting for eagles to fly."

Lily squeezed the sides of the boat while clenching her jaw. *Don't they know she's an angel and should be respected?* She flared her nostrils but knew she didn't want to argue with rude, smelly, long-eared men. Briella said nothing, so Lily stayed quiet too, even though she wanted to correct Finn.

Lily turned around. An image of her sixth grade social studies teacher at her previous school when her family lived in Florida came to mind. The large brute of a man, who also served as the football coach, flung students' folders back to them in class. Lily cringed when it was her turn to catch hers because if she didn't, loose papers would go flying. Finn was no better than him.

The dark silhouette of Atmos Island rose against the nighttime sky. Branches of fir trees covered the hilly terrain of the island. Pinpricks of light flashed into view and carved a path across the water of Gala Lake. Lily heard the sigh of water pass the wooden hull as they neared the dock. Under the light of blazing torches, Captain Grouse barked orders to Finn.

Lily scrambled out when they docked while Briella paid the captain.

The captain growled. "Next time, get here before dusk!"

Lily marched up the center of a moonlit road. "They were rude," she said to Briella when they were out of hearing range. "And I'm sorry for what they said about your butterflies."

Briella's butterflies rode on the angel peacefully. "Thank you."

Lily walked sideways and swatted the air. "They obviously don't know anything. I hope we *never* see them again!"

Briella stopped and faced Lily. "Never? Hmm... Everyone is on a journey, even Finn and Captain Grouse."

Lily stood confused. Hadn't her words cheered Briella up?

Briella glanced at a home made of stone at the top of the hill, light from its windows streaking across the road. "John's house is right up there. Is he ever going to be surprised!" Briella turned and walked up the dark road, Lily following.

Whiffs of wood smoke swirled in the chilly evening air as they approached John's house. Briella knocked on a heavy wooden door and a middle-aged man answered. His lamblike ears extended from both sides of his head through brown hair. His red sweater was buttoned and he wore corduroy pants and slippers.

"Greetings, John!"

"Greetings, Briella. What brings you out tonight?" His warm expression glanced from Briella to Lily.

"Wonderful news: The eagles have flown!"

His gentle look changed to a penetrating stare. "What did you say?"

Briella spoke with a bubbly voice. "We have in our company Miss Lily Lightfoot." Briella leaned into John. "She came here by way of *the lamb*."

John became very serious. He inspected Lily as if looking through a microscope in science class. He looked back at Briella. "She has seen the *lamb*?"

"Yes."

His eyes widened and he put his hands over his heart. His mouth dropped open followed by a delightful smile that spread across his face.

"May we come in?" asked Briella.

John staggered backwards. "Of course, yes! Please, come in!" He watched Lily follow Briella.

"May I take your coat and scarf, Miss Lightfoot?" asked John, his face beaming.

Lily handed them to him and he draped them on a chair. She took off her boots while Briella removed hers.

"Come in." He led the way into a rustic main room with dark wood trim and patted a comfortable chair. "You're welcome to sit here, Miss Lightfoot."

"Thank you, sir. You can call me Lily, sir."

"All right." His brown eyes dazzled in the firelight. "And you can call me John."

Lily sunk into the soft leather chair in front of a crackling fire and felt its warmth on her face.

Briella touched Lily's shoulder. "Enjoy the fire. We'll be right back."

Two small butterflies from the back of Briella's head flew to a table beside Lily, their black wings fluttering rapidly. Their long tails with white markings spiraled behind them as if they were in front of a fan.

In the mesmerizing movement of their tails, Lily rehashed the day's events in her mind. She could hardly believe the chorus concert was earlier that day. And that she had talked with her mom on the porch. *I wonder if she's called the police by now?* The crackle of the fire and the spinning butterfly tails made her yawn.

"I hope the dragon tails are not putting you to sleep." Briella said as she placed a tray on the table. The small fliers flew back to Briella's head, completing her tiara.

Lily perked up. "Oh, no. They're awesome."

Briella handed Lily a slice of apple pie sprinkled with cinnamon. "I agree."

Lily placed the plate on her lap. "Are you sure my parents aren't worried?"

"As I have already said, they are not worried. It is as if time is frozen in your world. When you go back, you will resume right where you left off. Trust me."

Although that was peculiar, Lily believed Briella and was at ease with her. Hungry, she took a bite of the pie. "This is delicious!"

John's eyes twinkled as he poured tea and pulled up a chair next to her. He reminded Lily of her father and grandfather, all rolled into one person. "I'm glad you like it. We've waited a long time for the appearance of the lamb. Those who have ears to hear, let them hear!"

Briella took a bite of her dessert. "I think the ears are the finest feature of the inhabitants of Whule."

Lily reached for her cup and took a sip while running a finger along the edging of the cushion. She wrestled with figuring out how to ask a delicate question without sounding rude. She mustered up courage. "I don't want to sound rude but why are your ears so big?"

"Why?" John leaned back in his chair. "That's simple. The people of this world are made in the image of their creator." John rested his hands on his lap. "And I know you know who that is."

John's penetrating eyes fixed on Lily. His serious expression gained all her attention, and she dared not blink. And her heart rate pounded in her neck. She wasn't sure why. She whispered, "I do?"

John's stern face softened with a smile as light from the fireplace reflected in his eyes. "Yes, you do. Did you see the lamb today?"

Lily gave a small nod.

"Then, you saw our creator."

Chapter Four

Where Love Dwells

The bumpy-faced vulture screeched his arrival as he carved his way over the Dreading Mountains that lined the backside of Sapphira's Wasteland. He spiraled downward through black smoke rising from a tower, averting his flight pattern to avoid hungry dragons lunging from the rocky range in search of their next meal.

He flew to the castle guarded by thick-scaled dragons and glided through an opened door decorated with bones. Dodging brandished maces of large trolls, he sliced through the dark throne room. His eardrums vibrated at the scratching sounds of centipedes that crawled up pillars in the dank hall.

Swooping in, he touched down and bowed before his master, proud of this very moment for which he had lived his entire life.

The red gown of Sapphira the Sorceress draped to the topmost step of a staircase made of bones. A large red stone centered in a crown of four-inch-long pointy teeth reflected flames from torches. From her chair of power, her garnet-glazed eyes fixed on the vulture.

"Speak," she commanded in a gravelly voice.

The vulture lifted his head and loudly announced: "Your Majesty, the eagles have flown!" Then he bowed, touching the ground with his beak.

Deep silence rooted in the hall. No scurrying insects or breathy trolls could be heard. Sapphira lifted a hand to a guard near the base of the staircase as the vulture's left eyelid twitched.

Sapphira growled at the guard. "Kill him."

***

Thump, thump, thump.

Lily stirred in the morning sunlight. In the waking haze, she remembered eating apple pie with Briella and John by the fire, talking about her world and answering questions.

Thump, thump, thump.

Lily propped herself up in bed and shielded her eyes. The lamb's silhouette formed in the bright light on the other side of the window. He tapped again with his head.

Thump, thump, thump.

With a smile on her face, Lily flung the quilted blanket

aside, got dressed, and made the bed quickly. She pulled on her boots by John's front door and hurried outside.

The lamb pranced down a path that zigzagged through maple trees. Lily ran after him, passing sap buckets that dangled from hooks on their trunks. A view of Gala Lake and Lambstone Mountain rose up before her. The lamb climbed up a large rock and lay down. Lily climbed up and faced him.

"Baa." The lamb nestled next to Lily.

"So, here you are again." She stroked the back of his head. He nuzzled his nose into her elbow. Lily paused. "Hey, how did you get over here anyways?"

"Baa."

"I'm sorry but I don't speak lamb." She felt the soft hair inside one of his ears. "But I wonder if you are able to understand me."

The lamb rested his head on her thigh, and she put her arm around him feeling warmth.

Across the lake, Lily squinted at Lambstone Mountain as the morning sunlight beamed on the white sheer rock surface. Birds flew in her line of sight and the sound of water lapped on the shore beneath her. Time slowed in the gentle breeze. Lily could have stayed there in that peaceful moment with no worries forever.

Lily rubbed the fleece on the back of the lamb's neck. "I think there might be something special about you."

John's voice called through the trees. "Lily? Are you out here?"

"I'd better go. I'll be right back."

She climbed off the rock, skirted around a couple of maple trees, and found John on the path, his brow wrinkled.

"Is everything all right?"

"Sure."

"Why are you out here all alone?"

"I'm not alone. I'm here with the lamb."

John's ears perked forward. "The lamb? Where?"

"Over there." When Lily pointed in the direction, John

walked fast to the rock, Lily keeping up beside him. But when they got there, the lamb was gone. "He *was* here."

John smiled at Lily as a breeze ruffled his brown hair. Then, his expression turned serious before he turned to look over Gala Lake. "Oh, I believe you. Elstar will come and go as he pleases. The time draws near when we will see him …" he turned to Lily, "…face to face. But that time is not yet."

Elstar?

Lily repeated the name to herself. *Elstar. But wait. Last night, didn't I hear that the lamb was their creator? I was so tired but I'm sure I heard that.*

John took a deep breath in and let it out then proceeded to a nearby hanging sap bucket. He lifted the cover, looked inside, took the bucket off the hook, and glanced back at Lily. "Those who have ears to hear, let them hear."

The slosh of the maple syrup in the bucket stirred Lily's understanding. What was it John just said? There was something familiar about the phrase. He had said it the night before. 'Those who have ears to hear'? Lily was miles away. Yes, it was that those words were the words of Jesus Christ, the Son of God. John looked like he was talking. His lips moved and his hair ruffled again above his lamblike ears from another light breeze. Her apparent blank stare must have caused him to realize she missed what he said.

"I said, you must be hungry. Let's go into the house and have breakfast and we can talk more."

Lily slowly nodded to John then glanced around, curious why the lamb had disappeared.

John set the bucket of raw syrup on the stone step outside his door before holding the entrance open for Lily.

At the kitchen stove, John stirred maple syrup into a pan. "The secret to great oatmeal is to pour the maple syrup, which has been boiled down to perfection by yours truly"—he pointed to himself with bright eyes—"into the pot of water and let it heat up *before* adding the oatmeal. Now, if you would reach into that cupboard for two bowls and place them on the table there with the napkins, we'll be set for breakfast."

Lily obeyed as John pumped water from a pitcher pump, filled two cups, and poured the oatmeal.

John sat down at the table motioning Lily to join him. "I don't know if you've noticed but Briella left in the middle of the night."

Lily pulled out a chair and sat down, her eye drawn to a red candle-like object on the table. "I didn't know."

The red candle with a gold base matched the red in John's sweater. As Lily looked at the centerpiece, she didn't think it was a candle after all. There was no wick. The object was similar to a cross only with a coat hanger on top.

John folded his hands. "Let's pray."

Lily bowed her head. John's prayer reminded her of how her father prayed.

When he finished praying, John poured more syrup on his oatmeal from a small pitcher and cream from another pitcher. "You can never have too much syrup. Help yourself, if you like. Briella has gone to gather friends for our journey and line up a sailboat. Have you ever sailed before?"

"No."

"Well, we're sailing today on a fine cutter sailboat. Should fly across Gala Lake, if the wind is right!" John swooshed his arm then rested it on the table.

At ease with John, Lily smiled at his warm-hearted ways. She could tell he was a good man who only meant kindness and goodness to others.

"You know," he said, "you are the only person in this world with short ears—except for Briella."

Lily wiped the corners of her mouth with a napkin, curious about that. "Why does she have short ears?"

"Now that's a good question. I don't rightly know. But I will tell you this—her devotion on Lambstone Mountain over the years has been admirable. I have found her to be a great comfort in our wait for the appearance of the lamb."

"How long have you been waiting?"

"Thousands and thousands of years. I, myself, have only been waiting fifty years, not near as long as Briella." John scraped out the rest of his oatmeal. "But the wait is over. Let's be on our way!"

He tossed his dirty dishes in the sink. "Just set your bowl, cup and spoon here. Since the end times are here, there's really no need to wash them!"

Lily finished the last of her oatmeal, slugged down the water in her cup, and set her dishes in the sink next to John's. With coats and scarves in hand, they strode out the front door, Lily trying to keep up with John's lively step while warding off nagging questions about the end times.

**

A sailboat with *The Gallant* written across the back rocked on the waves of Gala Lake, its mast swaying beneath a cobalt blue sky. Sunlight bounced on the windows of a small cabin centered on the deck to Briella standing on the dock. Two women and a man talked with her beneath the brightly-colored wings of fluttering butterflies.

"Good morning!" said Briella to Lily and John. "What a beautiful day to embark upon our journey! The finest of friends go with us. Let me introduce you. First, here is Hannah."

Large white ears protruded through tousled gray curls on an older, short woman who looked as if she could have been anyone's favorite grandmother. Hannah wore a rumpled coat of yellow and a large cloth bag dangled from her arm. She reached out to shake Lily's hand. "What a joy it is to meet you, my dear!"

Shaking her hand, Lily replied, "Thank you. It's nice to meet you too." Hannah and John exchanged nods as if they already knew each other.

"And may I introduce Deborah," said Briella.

The smooth strands of Deborah's blond hair could not possibly conceal her large, black-tipped ears. Dressed in a tailored coat of blue, the younger, taller woman said, "Welcome, Lily. May peace rest upon you this lovely morning."

Lily shook her outstretched hand. "Thank you. And to you."

Briella rested her hand on the shoulder of a man with a beard. "And here is Job, come from his estate in Ephra."

53

"Hullo, Hullo! Greetings to you!" Job's robust voice echoed down the dock. His brown lamblike ears matched a beard that hung over the collar of a brown tweed jacket. He threw his arms around Lily in a hug and then held her in front of him. "I said to myself, this has got to be the best morning of my life, one I have waited for for a long time! Welcome, young lady. Welcome, indeed!"

Lily's cheeks grew warm from embarrassment. "Yes, well, okay." She nodded, not sure what to say. "Thank you."

"John," said Job, "you're looking fairly chipper this morning!"

"I'm feeling it too, my friend," replied John.

Hannah extended her arms. "Now that we are all introduced, let's begin with prayer."

On the dock beside the sailboat, Lily's friends bowed their heads and prayed for safety, provision, and courage to endure to the very end.

Job clapped his hands. "Amen. So be it. Let's be on our way!"

Lily put her coat and scarf on and followed her long-eared friends onto the sailboat. She grasped rope railings as she balanced herself across the gangway.

Once on board, the captain tipped a welcome with his hat. Lily was glad to see he was not Captain Grouse. The captain directed the group to the back of the boat. Lily stepped over ropes, steadied herself against the wall of the cabin as the boat rocked, then toppled forward into a long-eared man coming around the cabin's corner.

Finn.

She backed up and tripped over the rope. But Job caught her from behind and helped her regain balance.

Finn snapped. "Why don't you watch where you're going? Oh! It's *you!*"

Lily gawked. *Him?*

"No harm done. Let's get to our seat," said Job, taking Lily's arm.

Why does he have to be here? I'm going to make sure I stay far away from him! But as she walked past him, something was different. He still wore his dirty jacket with stains but his face and hair had been washed.

Hannah patted the space next to her on a long bench at the back of the boat. "Sit here, Lily."

Job escorted Lily to the bench where she took her seat between Hannah and Briella. Job pointed to a banner at the top of the mast waving briskly in the breeze. "Look at that wimple. A windy day today. There will be white caps on Gala Lake."

John looked up from peering over the railing. "We should make good time to Bethem."

Deborah buttoned up her coat. "Bethem? I thought we were going to Jerul?"

"We are," said Job. "But first, Bethem. This journey will need all nine of our closest friends."

"Hoist the sail!" the captain ordered.

Crewman cranked wheels attached to ropes to lift a purple sail to the top of the mast, like a flag being raised at the school's flagpole, and the cloth filled with air. *The Gallant* moved away from Atmos Island, the wind pulling the boat into the deeper waters of Gala Lake.

On a strand of Briella's white hair, one of the white butterflies flew in front of Lily's face. "How do they stay on?"

Briella grinned. "Their feet are stronger than you think."

"I guess so." Lily looked closer. "Are its legs hairy?"

"Yes. That's the Great White Mountain Flier, and the nectar of flowers gives them strong feet. There is always a time for the blooming of a flower," she tilted her head at Lily.

Briella's words comforted Lily as she looked across the lake at farmer's fields, homes, and barns similar to her world.

I'm far away from home and yet not so far.

If she were home, she'd be sleeping in, like every Saturday. Then, she'd practice the piano for her lesson on Tuesday and maybe with her father who played the baritone. He was a talented musician, also playing the trombone, tuba, piano, guitar, and even the banjo. He had said when she was ready, they would play special music in church together.

But here she was sailing, and not terribly concerned, although she didn't know why they were going to Jerul. She turned to Hannah and asked that very question.

"To see the king and queen and prepare for the end times. There will be a great feast. People will come from every direction." Hannah closed her eyes. "I look forward to seeing old friends."

Job lifted the collar of his tweed jacket. "And making new ones."

"And, meeting our namesakes," added Hannah.

Job chuckled. "Ha! I can't wait to meet that fella. I'm sure we'll have a few laughs together."

Hannah smiled at Lily. "We set our sights on grander times. We count on tomorrow and wish for the days to come. We have so much more than this. It is an honor to grace the now by believing that the time to come is worth so much more. This journey will prove valuable to you. We are your friends and we will be with you."

Hannah's words brought a smile to Lily's face.

After a time, Deborah's skin color turned pale. She forced a smile before crossing her arms over her stomach. "I'm sorry but I guess I'm not good at sailing. I think I'm getting sick. I've got a queasy stomach. Maybe if I go in the cabin, I'll feel better."

"Oh dear! You never did have sea legs." Hannah held Deborah's arm and the two of them staggered to the cabin door.

The captain approached John and Job. "Excuse me, sirs. I need to speak with you both." John and Job left with the captain.

"I need to check something, Lily," said Briella.

Alone on the bench, Lily looked behind the boat, rested her arm on the railing, and watched the foamy wake trail behind. *How long will this journey be?*

As waves crisscrossed behind, Finn slid in beside her. He flicked her ear with his finger.

Lily jerked her head back and clapped a hand over her ear while snarling her upper lip.

Finn spouted. "How come your ears are so short? They are ears, aren't they?"

"My ears aren't short. And I think you can get away from me now." Lily's sharp tone spewed from her mouth.

Finn leaned back. His small, mean eyes penetrated like daggers. "I've never seen ears like that before. Very odd."

Lily's heart thumped against her ribs. She scanned the area for her friends but no one was in sight.

Finn sneered. "You do realize that butterfly woman is nuts." He paused, looking Lily over. "Who are you? What shell have you been living in?"

"I haven't been living in a shell."

Finn wiped his nose on his sleeve. "Look at you, sitting there soaking up all their tripe."

Tripe? What's that? Well, whatever it is, I've got to get away from this man, that is, if he is a man.

Lily stood up, turned, and plowed into John who was returning.

"Is everything all right here?"

Finn was quick to reply. "Yes sir." Then he stood and sauntered away.

Lily stared after him. "No. Everything is not all right."

John touched Lily's arm and warmth spread through her body. They sat together on the bench. "He is a rough character," said John. "That's for sure."

"Yesterday, when he and Captain Grouse rowed Briella and me to Atmos Island, he said he wanted to destroy all the butterflies."

"Hmm, I'd like to see him try. They're not normal butterflies, as you may have noticed." John dipped his head and his bright eyes drew out a smile from Lily.

John looked to where Finn had walked away. "Briella is not the one in danger. And you are not either. I and the others will watch over you. It's Finn who is in great danger. I hope he comes to his senses before it's too late. I'd hate to see him go to the Abyss." John looked back at Lily. "Did you know that it's to your glory to overlook an offense?"

Lily studied John's face. *Overlook an offense? Do you mean ignore the bad things that Finn says and does? I thought I was supposed to be of extreme importance.* She shook her head.

"Well, it is. We may have lost track of how many times offenses have been overlooked but our creator hasn't. He sees all. I'm here to say that love never fails. Those who have ears to hear, let them hear."

Lily stared across the water, taking in John's words. *Love Finn?* She twisted her mouth. *I don't even like him.*

Thin clouds scudded across the blue sky except where dark clouds hung over the mountain in the distance. A strong gust of wind surged the boat forward. Lily and John gripped the bench as a wave kicked up on Gala Lake.

John looked to the front of the boat. "Hannah is having a jolly time in the bow. Don't let her old age fool you. Let's hear what she has to say."

Lily followed John while grasping the railing. They stumbled into seats by Hannah, whose gray curly hair was now dripping wet.

"Woo hoo! We're sailing now!" Hannah laughed, holding a rope slanting from the mast as the sailboat dropped beneath them. For an older lady, she was fearless, riding the turbulent waves of Gala Lake, which rocked *The Gallant* like a huge see-saw. "One of life's sweetest joys," called Hannah as she faced into the wind, "is to roll over the waves!"

The big purple sail caught wind and pulled *The Gallant* over another wave and then dipped into the aftermath. Lily grabbed Hannah's arm as cold spray hit her in the face. "Whoa!"

Another wave toppled John, who called out, "At this pace, we'll sail right into Jerul!"

"Or maybe that sail will rip!" Finn's voice cut through the wind. He grasped the ladder affixed to the cabin.

Lily looked at the sail, trying to see if there were any rips.

"Woo!" Hannah yelled again. "Here comes another one. Hold on!"

Finn continued. "Your trip is a waste of time!"

"The end is coming, Finn," Hannah returned. "I was there at your beginning, when you were a baby boy. I'd like to be there at your end to share what's next!" Hannah faced Lily and tapped her nose with her index finger. "He was a joy to his parents. Nothing can take joy out of the heart."

Finn, a baby boy? Why is Hannah telling me Finn was a baby boy?

Finn pointed to the dark clouds over the distant mountains and called out over the waves, "That dark sky might! What is it? A huge forest fire? A field of burning tires? Or maybe it's the scary sorceress, Sapphira." He puckered his lips and wiggled his fingers in front of his face like a boogie man.

60

Hannah yelled back, "Where there's smoke, there's fire! Even so, promises made by our creator always come true. Know joy, know strength! But no joy, no strength. And a prayer request can turn sorrow into joy as sure as a man grows from a baby."

Memories of holding a baby entered Lily's mind. The smell of the baby's head and soft, little fingers that she held in her hand and would someday become a grown-up's made Lily look at the unruly, scowling man. Lily had to agree with Hannah. *Yes. Even Finn was once a baby boy.*

The Gallant rocked less and less as the wind died, like the end of a rollercoaster ride until the ride stopped. Hannah pointed to Deborah and Job sitting on top of the cabin. "Look at those two up there. My dear, why don't you visit them and hear what they have to say? There's a ladder to the roof."

Lily did as Hannah directed. With careful footing, she climbed up to the roof of the cabin. She found Deborah and Job leaning back on the ship's mast, their coats over their laps.

Job looked up, his bushy eyebrows lifted. "Hi there, young lady. Come sit with us." Lily fanned her coat out behind her and sat cross-legged.

Job pointed to the big purple sail that hung lifeless above them and then to the shoreline. "This here's what you call a 'dead calm.' There is the village of Bethem on the shore. See it? And Jerul is not far. But here we wait for the wind to pick up again, dead in the water. Mighty unusual weather we're having, huh?"

"I'd say." Lily squinted in the sunshine to see homes in the village of Bethem stretched down to the water's edge.

61

Deborah's once neat hair was now straggled by the wind. "How are you fairing?"

"I'm well." Lily paused. "And you? Are you feeling any better?"

"Yes, thank you. It takes me a while to get my sea legs, as they say, even though this is a lake. That last bit of turbulence was incredible. But now, we can see our destination. I know it's not long before we'll be on dry ground." Deborah rested her head against the mast and closed her eyes. The noonday sun shone on her peaceful face and black-tipped ears. She let out a sigh. "In the Realm, I won't have sea sickness. Or lengthy court cases to deal with. I long for the days of endless peace and no longer being a judge."

"It's all coming to an end," said Job. "I won't have to deal with the two-hundred-year-old apple press on my estate. It needs a new pulley wheel, and getting that old, rusty one off will be like putting socks on a rooster!"

Deborah chuckled then smiled. "May the faithful be like the sun when it rises in its strength."

There was no shade from the hot sun blaring down onto the boat. Job rolled up his shirt sleeves exposing tanned, beefy forearms. "They will. Elstar can do all things—he who set the foundation of Whule and marked off its dimensions. He will restore peace."

Lily ran a thumb across the suede on her boots. "He must be very powerful."

"No one is more powerful than the creator."

"That's true," agreed Lily.

Job's jolly amber eyes aimed warmth as good as the sun shining through a jar of honey. "Through hardship, I have realized our creator's providence. I said to myself, temperance brought patience. Now, I am richly blessed with a large family and estate, and splendid future, I might add."

Deborah lifted her head and her black-tipped ears sprang up. "I hear you like music, Lily. Do you sing?"

"Yes."

"I love songs of peace and patience. These last days can be endured better when we sing these kinds of songs."

The blue water of Gala Lake beyond the cabin roof shimmered peaceful as if in an echo of a dream. A picture of Lily's best friend Ada came to mind. They loved to sing together in church, sitting near the front on the piano side of the sanctuary.

"What do you think you will do in the Realm?" Deborah asked Job. "I can't see you retiring from the apple orchard business."

"Retire? Me? Farming's in my blood!" Job smacked his knee. "But this bum knee holds me back."

Deborah smiled. "It won't for long. The day of restoration approaches. You'll have a new knee."

Lily thought of Heaven, the place Jesus had gone to prepare for her. It would be a beautiful place with no hardships or bum knees.

Deborah nodded to someone behind Lily. "Hello, Finn."

Finn's head popped into view as he finished climbing the ladder. "Hello."

"Join us," said Deborah.

Finn sat down on the edge of the roof, leaning against the top portion of the ladder with his arms crossed. "What's with the weather?"

"Don't know," said Job. "I remember a time when the wind died down just before a violent storm. I had to get my saplings supported quick."

Finn cocked his head. "Yeah, well, you wouldn't want those little trees snapping."

"No indeed," agreed Job.

While Finn picked at a hole in his jacket, something nudged inside Lily's heart from hearing the words spoken by her friends. She asked herself questions. Had Finn ever had peace? Or if he did, had he forgotten about it? Or patience? Would there be anything in his heart to make him patient? While studying him, Lily grew in her understanding that it would be most unpleasant to have no peace and no patience.

Finn looked up with an ugly twist on his mouth. "I overheard you talking and I'm sorry to burst your bubble but there's no creator who created the foundation of Whule."

Job rested his hands in his lap. He took a deep breath and let it out. "How do you know?"

Finn cut in curtly. "Because every book ever written says we evolved. I only say this because I feel sorry for you all."

Job asked Lily, "Do you have this thought, Lily?"

Lily met Job's eyes. "What?"

"Do you believe in evolution?"

Lily made a silly face, the kind of silly face that everyone knows evolution is stupid. "No."

"I don't either. A bunch of nonsense! The Old Text states

we were created by EL." Then he looked at Finn. "So not every book says we evolved."

Finn's face grew red. He pointed at Job and raised his voice. "You know nothing, old man!"

Heat flushed through Lily's body. *How dare Finn speak to Job like that!*

Finn glared at Lily. "Who is this strange girl with weird ears? Are you the only one who saw the lamb?"

Lily's throat constricted. She tamped down any response. She wasn't going to be the focus of an irate man and get into an argument with him.

Finn continued. "How come you're the only one who's seen the lamb?" But then he glared at something behind her.

Wondering why she was a target and swallowing what felt like sandpaper, Lily squeaked out, "I don't know."

A dark cloud rolled overhead and a large shadow covered the boat.

Finn swore. His eyes fixed on something and his face turned white.

Lily turned to see what Finn was looking at.

"Brace yourselves, everyone!" the captain yelled from below. "We're about to be hit!"

Chapter Five

And Friendship Grows

"They're coming in fast!" The captain's voice boomed across the deck while Finn scrambled down the ladder.

Rowing directly at them under a dark cloud, the sight of a large ship with a dragon head and curved tail—like a Viking ship from medieval times—sent shockwaves through Lily's body. Four green-skinned beasts with tusks rowed at oars with incredible force. Her chest tightened when she saw a scary commander with a vulture on his shoulder. He yelled from a platform above the beasts, "Fire!" Men lit black cannons on either side of the ship's bow.

Job braced himself against the ship's mast. "Hold on!"

Deborah rolled onto her stomach and clenched the edge of the cabin's roof. "Get down, Lily!"

Lily dropped to her knees and flattened on her stomach. She grabbed the roof edge next to Deborah as the sailboat lurched beneath them to the sound of splintering wood. When the railing of the sailboat plunged beneath the water sending waves shooting across the deck, Lily locked her arms and legs as tight as she could.

The Gallant jerked from the force of another direct hit. Lily's legs rolled to the left, slamming into Deborah. Then they rolled to the right. She braced herself with her foot and tightened her grip, tucking her head between her arms and shutting her eyes. "They're going to sink us for sure! I thought Briella said nothing bad was going to happen to me!"

The ship righted, and taking a big breath and holding it, Lily looked up.

"It's not over yet!" yelled Job.

Deborah pointed. "Yes, look!"

Briella flew into the air between the boats. Her white hair grew brighter than usual. Each butterfly took an end section of her hair and flew frantically in place to form a circle around her head. Hovering in the air, Briella picked a flower from her pouch and flung it. The soft bloom instantly turned into a sharp spear of lightning, the spear lodging deep into a wooden plank on the ship's deck beside one of the green beasts. Fire ignited.

"Put it out!" shouted the commander, the vulture on his shoulder flailing its wings.

Fire spread up the beast's leg. With a mighty roar, the beast threw the oars down and beat his chest, trying to put the fire out. Men with buckets ran across the deck and threw water on the large creature but the fire kept burning. With the fire now on his face, the beast squealed, shook its arms, and threw himself into Gala Lake. Flames and smoke trailed behind as he sunk in the water.

Lily's eyes widened at the intense gaze on Briella's face before she turned and hurled another spear and then another. The men kept tossing buckets of water on the fire and stomping on the flames but they could not put out the raging fire. They rolled on the deck, wailing in agony, trying to snuff the flames but they continued to burn.

The fire raced to the mast and the scary commander. "You will die, Briella the White!" he yelled, shaking his fist at her as the vulture flew off his shoulder.

The commander's flaming torso and blazing ship sank beneath the water's surface, still burning, descending through dark swirls of water until it disappeared into the depths of Gala Lake.

Deborah's black-tipped ears drooped forward as she peered over the edge. "They hated us."

The vulture screeched overhead, circled, and flew toward the distant dark sky.

Briella flew back into the sailboat, her hair and butterflies settling back into place. She looked over the railing and said, "No, vile one, I will not die." She swiped her hands as if brushing off dirt and then gave a fiery look at Lily.

Lily froze. But when Briella grinned at her, a warm glow grew within Lily. She grinned back, convinced there wasn't anything frilly about an armed angel.

The way Briella brushed off her hands reminded Lily of her mother when she'd brushed off her hands from planting flowers. The grin that warmed her heart assured her of the safety Briella had guaranteed on Lambstone Mountain.

Job offered a hand to Lily. "We are safe now. Those evil men of Si are no longer. They will not be bothering us anymore, let me tell you."

With wobbly knees, Lily stood and planted her feet as solid as she could.

Below, the captain barked orders. "Get the crowbar! Grab hammer and nails! Finn, don't just stand there! Get the buckets! We're sinking!"

"We'd better help." Job hurried down the ladder. Deborah and Lily followed.

At the bottom of the ladder, Lily stepped into lake water, soaking her boots, but that was the least of the problems facing the crew of *The Gallant*. A crewman ripped boards from the cabin wall with a crowbar and threw them down the stairs inside the cabin. Another crewman hammered below deck.

The captain yelled, "Hurry up!"

Crewmen scurried to form an assembly line and Lily stepped in, passing a bucket of water from John to Deborah, who passed it to Finn, who passed it to Job, who dumped the water over the railing and returned the empty bucket to Hannah. Briella stood guard. They were making progress, but barely.

Over the sound of splashing water, Lily heard a man's robust voice. "Are you all right? Is anyone hurt? We came as fast as we could!"

70

The captain looked up. "Who's there?"

A slim, fit man wearing a uniform with pink stripes on his shoulders peered from around the corner of the cabin. His dark skin and hair matched his dark lamblike ears. "Joseph with the patrol guard, sir. Is everyone safe?"

"Yes," the captain replied, "but we're sinking."

"We'll help and tow you to Bethem," said Joseph.

"Excellent! I didn't hear your tugboat arrive. Great to know the patrol guard is here when you need them."

"We aim to serve but only wished we could have arrived sooner to prevent this horrific attack. We saw the whole thing," Joseph turned to Briella, "including you. You must be Briella the White."

Briella's butterflies fluttered around her face. "I am. Welcome aboard, Joseph."

***

The patrol guard tugboat towed *The Gallant* into the harbor at Bethem. Finn tied the damaged boat to the dock. When Hannah passed by, Finn asked, "Where's your joy now?"

"I still have it," said Hannah, smiling kindly to Finn. "We didn't sink." She steadied herself and stepped off the boat, Joseph behind her.

Lily followed Joseph then jumped onto the dock, spun around, and walked backward as she watched John, Job, Deborah, and Briella disembark. She punched the air with her fist. "Am I glad we survived that!"

Job laughed as he walked along the dock. "To think that commander said we'd die. Ha! No evil stands a chance against us."

Lily caught her boot on an uneven board and toppled backward but Joseph caught her.

"Easy there," he said. "You'd better walk forward or you'll be waterlogged."

Lily laughed. "You're right!" She turned to walk forward, following Joseph. "My boots are already sopping wet. Don't need to fall in and be totally soaked! But did you see those lightning bolts? And from flowers? Who would have thought? Nothing can stop an angel!"

"Well, yes. I told you no harm will befall you. Now, I know you are excited but try to tune your ears to wisdom, Lily," said Briella.

Lily stopped and let Briella catch up, peering into her dazzling eyes, Bluey flapping slowly above them. *Tune my ears to wisdom? What does that mean?* Lily nodded.

Briella addressed everyone. "Joseph will be a kind host while I go gather two more friends. I will return shortly." With butterflies swooping up and down behind her, Briella hurried down a side street, her white dress flowing.

Joseph waved his hand out in front of him and then indicated the direction in which they would go. "Please, this way. You are all invited to my home."

The small, thatched-roof stone cottages in the village of Bethem reminded Lily of the houses she had seen in drawings of old English villages in the sixteenth century. Most of the long-eared inhabitants ignored her and her friends except a few, who she believed heard the squishing and squashing of water inside her boots as she walked along the cobblestone road. Fragrant smells of flowers by windows and occasional whiffs of bacon passed under her nose.

When Joseph turned a corner, a stately-looking home with black columns across a porch filled the scene.

Lily gaped at the beautiful home. "You live here?"

Joseph nodded. The group followed him across the porch. He opened the door and welcomed everyone inside. "Please, come in. Feel free to remove your wet boots and set them on the hearth by the fire in the living room. I will get towels."

Lily removed her boots before entering a grand foyer with marble floors and a sweeping staircase. A painting hanging on the wall drew her eye. Unable to take her eyes off, she approached for a closer look, holding her boots.

Lily stood quiet. She stared at the painting, breathing softly. In the painting, under a dreary sky, a man with large ears hung upside down from a pole, his ankles punctured in a coat-hanger contraption. Blood stained his lifeless body and the ground beneath him.

Then, before her eyes, the scene changed to a familiar one—Golgotha, when Jesus Christ, the Son of God, the anointed, had died on the cross between two thieves hanging on either side of him.

Lily's heart pounded in her chest as she viewed the familiar scene. Her vision blurred from teary eyes. This was proof to her that God watched over her in this enchanted world. His presence was with her. Somehow, God had brought her into the world of Whule.

"Lily?" Hannah called from the living room.

Lily turned, realizing she was the only one in the foyer. She wiped her eyes then looked at the painting once more. It was as it was before. She blinked, breathed deep, and then entered the living room. Warmth caressed her face from a glowing fire in the fireplace. She sat on the sofa next to Hannah.

Hannah took off her socks. "I'm sorry if it gets a bit smelly in here but we should dry these out too."

Water sloshed in the bottom of Lily's boots.

"Just dump that water ..." Hannah looked around.

"... here." Joseph passed a bowl.

Lily dumped her boot water into the bowl and peeled off soaked socks, then added hers to the line in front of the fire. Joseph handed her a plush towel.

"Thank you." Lily wrapped it around her feet.

Hannah dabbed her feet. "How fortunate we were to have Briella help us. What an awful event! Goodness gracious."

"Indeed," said Job standing beside a grandfather clock. "But I said to myself, why couldn't she do something about that hole in the ship's hull?"

Deborah grinned.

With an iron rod, Joseph stirred the fire then added more wood. "In all my years of patrolling Gala Lake, there's never been anything like what we saw on its waters today." He faced everyone. "Last night, I had a dream, and in it, I was warned of the attack."

"Interesting," said John. "Our creator does speak through dreams sometimes."

Joseph nodded. "Very true. And I know now, the creatures we saw were part of Sapphira's Horde."

Hannah pulled an afghan over her lap. "Such horror. And did you see the ears of those men from Si?"

"Absolutely terrible," said John. Then he shook his head in sorrow.

"I've heard many people in the city of Si have done this horrible thing," Joseph continued. "They're doing it now in the royal city of Jerul. Evil is spreading."

Deborah cringed.

"They want to make a statement," said Job.

"And they have," added John. "But to their demise. They neither thank nor glorify EL." He looked at Lily and then sadly into the crackling fire.

The tick-tock of the grandfather clock resonated in its wooden cabinet. With a click, a tune played followed by the one o'clock clang. A long moment of silence followed.

Lily whispered to Hannah, "What did they do to their ears?"

Hannah patted Lily's shoulder. "My dear, they were cropped."

Cropped? What does that mean? A field trip to a farm back in the fourth grade came to Lily's mind. The cow's tails had been cropped for easier milking and to keep disease down. But people wouldn't chop off their ears, would they?

Deborah drew her knees to her chin. "It's awful. They cut off their ears, Lily."

Stunned, Lily imagined what her long-eared friends would look like, what her friends would have to endure to have such a procedure done.

"I'm so sorry for them. They do not want a loving creator to rule their heart," said Hannah.

"And then evil follows," said John, "and becomes their lord without them even aware. But have courage. Evil will be destroyed. We can count on that. Love is stronger than evil and we can count on blessings now and in the future."

"Yes, evil will be destroyed," said Deborah, her face cheery. "Our creator is very strong."

"Reason to be glad!" chimed Job.

Her friend's sure voices sent ripples of love through Lily's ears to her heart. She thought of her father when he bought her a beautiful long coat with a blue fox fur collar. She left the store walking on cloud nine, knowing her dad loved her very much, and very unaware of any evil in the world.

Lily's cheery moment was short-lived, however, when the silhouette of a long-eared man peered into the living room window, startling her. The stranger cupped his hands over his eyes in the outdoor sunlight making it hard for her to see who he was. Before she could tell anyone about him, a knock at the door sent Joseph to answer it. The stranger darted away.

Joseph returned with Briella holding a bag with bread sticking out. A girl wearing a purple poncho and holding a basket stood next to her. A man with a green bandana around his neck and a crate on his shoulder stood next to the girl.

Bluey and the white butterflies fluttered on Briella's head. "May I introduce Mary and Paul!"

***

Job searched a cupboard in the kitchen. "Have you any coffee, Joseph?"

Joseph opened a pantry door and handed Job a small sack.

"Ah, perfect! Thank you. I said to myself, a pot of coffee would be a fine thing to make."

Joseph nodded, his dark ears sprung back. "That would be fine, my friend."

"Thank you for your kind hospitality," said Hannah to Joseph.

"Of course." Joseph placed a stack of plates on a counter in the kitchen. "You are all my friends."

Around an island counter in the center of the kitchen, Lily and her friends made lunch. Deborah helped Paul empty the crate of meats and cheeses while Briella cut slices of bread, her butterflies flitting from one person to another.

"Can we help you unpack your basket?" Hannah asked Mary.

Mary's brown lamblike ears protruded from long black hair gathered to one side over her shoulder with a purple ribbon, which matched her purple poncho. "Yes, thank you." She handed a head of lettuce to Hannah and took four tomatoes from her basket, a jar of peppers, a jar of mustard, and a large onion. John began chopping the onion.

Mary handed Lily a tomato. "I'm glad we'll be traveling together. I like your ears, by the way."

"Thank you. I like yours too," said Lily, taking the tomato.

Mary leaned over the counter. "They're like Briella's. And I see they're not pierced."

Lily cut and added tomato slices to the platter, next to the shredded lettuce. She noticed Mary's weren't pierced either.

"Some girls have earrings all along the bottoms of their ears and across the tops and even at the point." Mary touched the ends of her lamblike ears.

"Men have pierced their ears too," said Deborah. She built a sandwich—spreading mustard, placing meat, cheese, lettuce, and tomato on two slices of bread and then bringing them together.

"I was such a man." Paul's brown hair swooped up at his large ears. He centered the green bandana around his neck. "I don't wear earrings anymore. Long story short—it's not for me." He picked up four glasses of lemonade and carried them into the adjacent dining room.

"So, how come your ears aren't pierced?" asked Mary.

"My dad won't let me get my ears pierced—not until I'm eighteen."

Mary put a banana pepper on her sandwich. "When you're eighteen, will you get them pierced?"

"It will probably hurt," said Job as he passed behind, carrying the coffee pot.

Lily grinned at Job. "Probably." She looked back at Mary. "I don't know."

Mary added lettuce to her sandwich. "Your father doesn't like it?" Mary tilted her head.

Lily had not given it much thought but accepted her father's rule. She didn't question it further. As she thought more, she wondered if her father's decision was based on a

Bible verse. She wondered if she would get her ears pierced at eighteen like other girls.

Mary leaned in. "I'm wondering: if your father doesn't like it, then maybe you shouldn't like it, out of respect for him."

Mary's brown eyes peered into Lily's. She had not thought of that before. Leaving her ears un-pierced could be a way to honor her father. Lily smiled at Mary, knowing that was a really good idea.

Everyone built their sandwiches the way they liked then carried them on plates to the table in the formal dining room. Except for Joseph, Briella, Mary, and Paul, everyone had bare feet because their socks and boots were still drying by the fire.

At the head of the table, Joseph prayed. As he prayed, Lily silently prayed.

Dear Lord, Thank you for watching over me in this world. Help me to have the ears to hear what you're telling me. Help me to tune my ears to wisdom. In Jesus' name.

"Amen." Joseph waved his hands over the table. "Please, everyone, eat."

After Job picked up his sandwich, Lily picked up hers and took a bite. And another. Then she drank half the lemonade. She picked an apple from the fruit bowl in the center of the table and took a bite.

"You were hungry!" Mary said to Lily.

Lily blushed. "Uh, I guess so. Sorry."

Paul took a peach from the bowl. "No worries! I've spent time in jail. They don't feed ya too good in there, especially that one in Rom. Short version of a long story, when I was

79

released, I ate a whole chicken, two potatoes, and a loaf of bread!"

Job chuckled. "Through it all, you endured."

"Faith. That's what I talk about, even in jail," said Paul. "Like all of you, I endeavor to honor my namesake."

Job pointed with his coffee cup to a picture hanging on the wall of a long-eared man with the word "Kindness" written beneath his image. "Like that fella. We know Joseph showed kindness to his brothers even after they threw him down a well, leaving him for dead. The story is recorded in the Old Text."

Joseph continued. "Yes, they wondered if he'd hold a grudge and pay them back. But he explained it was all part of EL's plan, intended for good. He dealt kindly with them and even forgave them."

Joseph's words stretched like roots into Lily's heart. She had heard this story before. Was this similar to the Joseph story she knew in the Bible?

Paul leaned back in his chair. "There's no law against kindness. We know our creator is the kindest."

Mary took green grapes from the fruit bowl. She turned to Lily. "You have seen the lamb, which makes you the spirit seer. Have you touched him?"

Spirit seer? Lily's thoughts whirled around as she let her eyes whirl around at her friends seated around the table.

Mary rested her chin on her hand with one elbow on the table. "What does he look like?"

"You don't know what a lamb looks like?" The words slid out of her mouth quicker than she meant, and she didn't mean

80

them. Lily bit her lip. Then she shook her leg. She couldn't take back what she already said. Had she ruined the hope of a lasting friendship?

But Mary touched her arm. "No, I don't," she said reassuringly. "Describe him."

Silence filled the room. They waited for Lily to say something. She looked at each of her friends and then at Mary. "I'm … I'm sorry for what I said."

Mary smiled. "It's okay. Tell us what he looks like."

Relieved by Mary's graciousness, Lily listed traits. "His fleece is super soft. And warm. He has a pink nose and ears. And dainty hooves. And a fluffy chest." She looked into Mary's brown eyes dazzling in the light coming through the window of the formal dining room. "And eyes like yours."

Mary beamed.

"I'm confused about something, though," said Lily. "How can I touch a spirit? I shouldn't be able to touch a spirit, should I?"

"The lamb is the spirit body," said Briella as the indigo-colored wings of the butterflies on her wrists opened and closed slowly. "Sometimes, the spirit takes the form of something. Do you understand this, Lily?"

Clueless, Lily shook her head.

"Like a dove?" suggested Briella.

A dove? Lily concentrated. Like when the Holy Spirit came down from Heaven in the form of a dove?

John set his empty plate aside. "Only the spirit seer can see the lamb. In our world, there is a prophecy written in the Old Text. We think you're the spirit seer."

81

"Me?"

John nodded.

Lily shook her head. "But I'm no one special."

John sat back in his chair and peered into Lily's eyes. "Are you sure about that? One cannot limit what a creator can do."

Chapter Six

Blessed with Nine Traits

A satisfied coo echoed over the glass-smooth marble floors of the royal hall in the Palace of Jerul. Perched on a gem-studded bird stand, Pity-Petty, the royal carrier pigeon, feasted on red grapes from a gold cup and then cleaned his feathers. Queen Esther unfolded the tiny note from his satchel. Her face radiated as she read the message. She announced to the court, "Make preparations! I have received the most excellent news! The eagles have flown! Elstar has appeared!"

***

After lunch, Lily strolled with her friends through rows of lavender in Joseph's fragrant formal back garden. The afternoon sun warmed them, keeping coats inside, and since their boots were still drying by the fire, everyone but Joseph, Mary, Paul and Briella walked the lanes with bare feet.

They came to four white benches with thick green yew bushes lining the backsides of the benches. Lily and Mary joined Deborah already there as the others talked nearby.

As sunlight fell on her black-tipped ears, Deborah sighed. "I could spend the whole afternoon here."

A simple arrangement at the end of a stone terrace in front of cedar trees filled the area. Shoots from a green vine with tiny white blossoms cascaded from a delicate ceramic planter in the shape of a well on top of a pedestal. Dark green myrtle carpeted the ground.

"I know what we saw today was disturbing but we must keep trusting our creator to bring us to the peaceful shore."

Deborah's voice soothed Lily until the moment was interrupted by a small sniff. Lily looked at Mary and Deborah. Neither one of them sniffed. Lily tilted her head and pinpointed a scuffing sound coming from the yew bush. Getting up to investigate, she saw a brown stone move under the bush. She stood still and stared at it until she realized it was not a stone but a boot. She pulled back a branch and found a long-eared man. Finn!

"What are you doing in there?"

"Sh. Keep your voice down," Finn whispered with a snap. "Don't tell anyone I'm here."

Lily hesitated. "Fine." She let the branch go and it smacked him in the face.

The next series of events happened quickly. A shrill whistle filled the air. Finn burst from the bush lunged headfirst into the pedestal. He sent the delicate planter flying into the air. It crashed onto the stone terrace and broke into many pieces.

A police officer busted through the cedar trees and grabbed Finn's arm. "Just a moment here! I've been watching you, but I got you now!"

Finn struggled to break free.

The officer tugged at his arm again. "Oh, not so fast. Why are you snooping around, hiding in bushes, and peering into Mr. Joseph's window?"

Finn frowned. "I ... was looking for a cat."

Lily could tell he made that up.

Deborah asked Lily, "Isn't that the crewman from *The Gallant?*"

Lily nodded.

"Looking for a cat, eh?" said the officer. "I don't think so. You're coming with me."

Joseph and the others drew near and Finn acknowledged them. "Hi! Thanks, man, for coming to the rescue. Pretty scary stuff on the lake but you patrol guards are on it!" Finn spoke as if he and Joseph were buddies.

When Joseph smiled, Finn put on as pleasant a face as he could. "I'm sorry. I wasn't looking and tripped. I'll pay for the damages."

Lily made a smug grin. *Really?*

The police officer forced Finn's steps. "I'll get him out of here." He turned and Finn obeyed.

But before Finn was led away, Lily locked eyes with him like a strong magnet to pieces of metal. Questions churned in her mind. *What made him follow them from the harbor? Was there a reason he was looking in the window and hiding in the bush?*

Lily surprised herself when she lifted her hand. "Wait."

The officer looked back, studying her.

Blood coursed through Lily's veins. She had accidently placed herself in the center of attention—not where she wanted to be. She looked around at her friends who all waited for her to speak. "Well, I mean … does he have to … go to jail?"

"Just a moment," said Joseph to the officer. He looked over the scattered debris on the terrace and then at Lily. "What should we do?"

He should go to jail. It might be good for him. He could sit there and think things over. Don't scoundrels need to go where scoundrels go? Lily slowly looked at Joseph. Why was he asking her what should be done?

In the clutches of the officer, Finn waited for a decision.

Lily's ears grew warm. Could her friends hear her heart beating in the quiet of the garden? She kept thinking of the word 'kindness' while looking at Joseph. Then she met John's eyes. His warning of Finn's danger returned to her mind.

In a soft voice, she asked, "Can you let him go?"

Joseph nodded to the officer and he released his hold of Finn's arm.

***

Lily stood beside Mary on the porch of Joseph's elegant home, her feet toasty warm from fire-dried socks and boots. She bit her lip, not sure if she had done the right thing. But Finn had politely thanked Joseph, turned, and began putting the broken pieces of the planter in his jacket which he held like an apron until Job found a box for him.

Lily and Mary watched two drivers steer two open carriages, each pulled by a horse, to the front of the house, drawn-out sneezes coming from the steeds at their halt. Lily breathed in the smell of hide and leather. The fancy carriages were the kind used for kings and queens with the tops folded down so passengers rode in the open air.

"Can we sit together?" Mary's purple poncho hung folded over her arm.

"Sure." Lily had gathered her hair to the side like Mary's. The wool coat and red scarf hung draped over her arm.

Finn came from around the house and placed the box with the broken pieces of the planter on the porch step. "Thanks for saving me from going to the can."

Lily half-smiled.

Finn put his hands in his pockets. "I never seen anything like it, that Briella. I mean, did she fly? I looked for wires." His smile wasn't too bad—a little odd, maybe, but no stranger than his ridiculous ears.

Lily tried to smile. "There aren't any. I already looked."

The front door swung open and Hannah stepped out. "I wanted to bring a copy of the Old Text." She patted her cloth bag then asked Finn, "Have you got your copy?"

Finn shifted his weight under the afternoon sun. "No, ma'am." He grimaced then opened his jacket with his hands still in the pockets. "Well, thank you all. I'll be on my way now. Got to get to Jerul before sundown. I'll be back to pay for the damages, I promise."

Lily was sure he had no intention of doing that.

Finn glanced at Joseph and then backed away, bowing, and turned toward the street.

"Jerul?" Mary descended the porch steps and stepped toward Finn. "That's where we're going. Are you going to walk there?"

Finn turned back around. "Well, yeah."

"We're going there. Would you like to ride with us?"

Finn hesitated. Then he cocked his head to the side. "Sure. I could do that."

Lily's eyes went wide. She hoped no one saw the grimace she made at Mary's suggestion.

Lily, Mary, Finn, Briella, John, and Paul entered the first open carriage. The rest boarded the second. The driver snapped the reins and Lily and her friends pulled away from Joseph's house with a jolt, the second carriage following. Lily felt like part of a royal family, except when she looked at Finn. *Had Mary been too friendly? Well, even royal families have problem members.*

John unbuttoned his red sweater. "We can be glad for this good weather."

Bluey swooped above the carriage and then settled back on Briella's forehead. "The weather holds. We should make good time to the royal city."

The warm afternoon sun fell on Lily's shoulders as they rode past quaint shops in the village of Bethem. Passersby waved to them in the open carriage and Mary waved back.

The gleam of the sun's rays reflected on the windows of a tea shop and then on Finn. Was his expression better? Or was it the way the sun shone?

Paul moved to the edge of his seat and quickly turned around. "That tea shop flies Sapphira's flag! Oh, what that flag represents! They will not have any of my business."

Lily looked back. A red flag flapped in the breeze but she couldn't make out the design on it since they had already passed the shop.

Finn rested his arm on the edge of the carriage. "Yeah, well, they're crazy." He spoke as if he knew first-hand then he looked at Briella sitting across from him. "But I think maybe you're not crazy."

Briella mused. "Oh? Then, you do not wish to strike my fluttery Lepidoptera, scoop up their tiny remains, and use them as fertilizer in your uncle's garden?"

Finn's face paled and he coughed while readjusting his sitting position. "Ah, well, no. Not anymore."

Bluey kept his wings open while Briella gazed at him with penetrating blue eyes. "That would be wise."

Finn gave a shaky laugh while trying to look pleasant with a fake smile. "But you know, I've never seen anyone fly before. You could make a lot of money! People would pay good money to see you fly."

Briella laughed. "What? I am not interested in making money."

Finn sat back, looking somewhat perplexed. He let his hand slap his thigh. "Everyone wants to make money."

A stern look came over Briella's face. "Paper currency is nothing to me. Its value is from the one who assigned it in this world. I serve the creator."

Finn drew his eyebrows together and then turned his head as the carriage passed the last home in Bethem. He mumbled something under his breath but Lily didn't hear what he said. Silence filled the carriage and only the horse's clip-clop could be heard as they made their way along the country road. Lily heard the others talking in the carriage behind them, Hannah and Job laughing.

After a few moments, John turned to Paul. "I've been thinking about your mission journeys at sea. What was the name of that ship you sailed on?"

A breeze blew through Paul's wavy hair and the green bandana around his neck flapped in the wind. "*The Malta.* I was on my way to face charges in the city of Rom when we were shipwrecked."

Mary combed her long black hair with her fingers. "You were shipwrecked? What happened?"

"A violent storm hit us. I had a close call with a shark but thankfully, it swam away. Long story short, after hours at sea, we reached the shore and kind people welcomed us."

"And your faith!" John turned to Finn. "And you, Finn. You've sailed before, haven't you?"

"Yup."

Mary asked Finn, "How long have you been a sailor?"

Out of nowhere, Finn snapped at Mary. "Too long!"

Lily glared at Finn. *How dare he talk to Mary like that! Mary was the one who offered him a ride.*

The group grew silent again until Finn pressed his hands together, touched his lips, and looked at Mary. "I'm … I'm sorry for that snap. I don't like talking about sailing. I shouldn't have snapped."

Mary nodded and then looked away.

Finn's disdained look melted a little as he pointed to the top of Briella's head. "I wouldn't mind talking about those butterflies, though."

Briella sat like a statue.

Was she going to tell him to get out of the carriage? Was she going to pick a small flower and zap him right between the eyes?

Briella asked, "What do you want to know?"

Finn cocked his head. "I don't know. Tell me about them."

"A butterfly is one of EL's most beautiful creations. A once mealy, low, caterpillar crawling on the ground can become a new creature flying high with a whole new view. My special butterflies represent nine characteristics."

Finn crossed his arms. "Nine characteristics?"

"Yes, of our creator." Briella pointed to the two red butterflies on her shoulders flapping simultaneously to the rhythm of a steady heartbeat. "The Red Majestics represent love, which never fails." Briella gave Lily a glance. "That 'never' *can* be said."

Lily agreed and smiled.

Briella then pointed to the yellow wings of the next butterflies on the edges of her shoulders. "Yellow is the perfect color for the Sunnyskips. Their joy overflows and gives strength for each day."

She pointed to the next set of butterflies on each part of her upper sleeve. "Here are the Blue Sapphires. Their dark blue wings represent peace which passes all understanding." Briella gave Finn a stern look and then continued.

"Next are the brown Leafwings. They represent patience. Even though they look like dead leaves when their wings are closed, they are very much alive, persevering to the end."

Mary leaned in. "They do look like dead leaves!"

"Yes." Briella then pointed to the next set of fliers, also on her upper sleeves. "The Black-Spotted Pink Swallowtails symbolize kindness, which should not be underestimated. On my elbows are the Purple Rosewings. They always fly for goodness, which is stronger than evil." She and Mary exchanged smiles.

Then Briella pointed to the lower part of her sleeves. "The green Olivewings fly steady for faithfulness. They waver not, even in the fiercest of storms." She grinned at Paul.

"Next are the orange Royal Monarchs, making gentleness their cause. And last, but not least, on my wrists are the indigo Tapertails beautifully displaying self-control. No trial is too great for them."

Finn sat quiet, holding his chin with his thumb. "Why do you have the same butterflies on each sleeve?"

"Balance," said Briella, matter-of-factly.

Finn smirked then pointed to the top of her head. "And what about those?"

"With Bluey in the front as the crowned jewel, two Blazing White Morphos, two Great White Mountain Fliers, and two Dragon Tails in the back are the seven butterflies that form my eternal tiara."

"And what do they stand for?" asked Finn.

"Eternity."

Bluey fluttered, causing a chain reaction for the others to flutter in the tiara and along her belled sleeves.

The nine traits Briella stated swooped around in Lily's mind. Love, joy, peace, patience, kindness, goodness, faithfulness, gentleness, and self-control? Had she heard these before? Yes! They were the nine fruits of the Holy Spirit. She remembered learning about them in Sunday school.

Finn put his finger to his nose and then shook it at Briella. "It's a clever trick you got there."

"It is no trick. They are what Elstar has given me."

"Elstar?" A corner of Finn's mouth raised up. "Yeah. Well, I know you are all Elstarians. But there's no way there's a creator. You have all been duped!" He held his eyebrows up. Then he continued as if debating for office. "The world is far too complicated. Do you know how many different kinds of species there are, each with their own unique features?"

Briella looked squarely at Finn.

Finn looked squarely back, then announced, "Elstar is nothing more than a fictional character."

Lily caught Paul's wide eyes.

John faced Finn. "But surely, it would take a grand designer to design all of creation. EL is that designer."

"Pfft!" Finn turned his head away from the group.

In silence again, except for the clip-clop of the horses, a song entered Lily's inner musical ear. She heard the melody and minor harmony and kept rhythm with the horses. The lyrics had the names El Elyon and El Shaddai. Her grandfather had explained EL was another name for God.

Lily met John's warm brown eyes and remembered what he said on *The Gallant*. Finn was the one in danger. She eyed Finn staring across a field, knowing he was the one who was duped.

As views of Gala Lake appeared through trees lining the road, Lily leaned her head back and gazed at patches of blue sky through overhanging branches of white blossoms on the trees. As they passed underneath, she breathed in the sweet fragrance and let soft petals brush her face.

Mary let the blossoms touch her face too.

John excitedly turned in his seat. "Here is the Cobblestone Church at Gala Lake! That means we're half way to Jerul."

Lily and Mary popped their heads up to see sunshine pour on the stained glass windows of the church and gleam on the steeple. Lily's eyes stopped on the cross-like device with the coat hanger on top. Was it the same contraption in the painting at Joseph's house? Was it the same table centerpiece on John's table?

"What's that?" asked Lily, pointing to the steeple.

Mary's long ears drooped on both sides of her head and she twirled an end piece of her hair. "That's the Gambrel. Elstar died on the Gambrel for us."

Lily inspected the device, her mind spinning. *Like Jesus dying on the cross for me? Is Elstar the anointed one, like Jesus? EL's Star?* Lily held still. Her eyes moved from left to right. An awareness of God's presence came over her. Was God viewing her through a huge magnifying glass from His home in Heaven? She looked across the waters of Gala Lake.

Mary spoke gently. "Lily, are you all right?"

The waves on Gala Lake tossed gently. Had the attack sprung up so quickly on such fine waters? *What's going on, God? Why am I here?*

Lily turned slowly back to Mary. "I'm all right. It's just—I'm wondering how much longer I'm going to be here."

"In two days time, you will return to your home," said Briella, "unless you wish to go home now."

The abrupt answer jarred Lily. "You mean I could go home right now?"

Briella nodded. "Yes, and return exactly at the time you left."

Mary said, "But I was just getting to know you. Please keep going. We're your friends. I'm your friend." She tugged Lily's arm as her face brightened. "Don't you want to see what will happen?"

Lily's confidence bolstered from the gleam in Mary's eyes.

"We will travel together and stay together to the end, don't you worry," said Mary, and then she added, "Elstar led you here. I know you can trust him."

"And have an opportunity to tune your ears to wisdom," added Briella.

Curiosity spiked Lily's interest. She did want to tune her ears to wisdom. She gave a small nod.

"Great!" said Mary. "It's going to end well. I'll be with you right to the end. You wait and see."

Finn rolled his eyes. "Pfft!"

John shaded his eyes. "Who are the two men standing there in the lake? Driver, would you stop?" The driver steered the carriage to the side of the road, the other carriage pulling up behind.

"The one wearing the orange shirt is Philip," said Briella getting out of the carriage. "He has much to add to our journey. Let's go down to the water's edge together and visit with him and his friend."

Lily followed Mary, scooting past Finn and leaving the carriage last. Seeing that Finn hadn't moved, she turned back. "Aren't you coming?"

Finn leaned his head back in his hands cradled by interlocking fingers. "I'm not going anywhere. Just going to sit here and wait for my ride." He sprawled his legs out and closed his eyes. "Hurry along. Catch up with your little friends."

A scowl formed on Lily's face. "They're not little."

Finn snorted. "Your little weird friends."

Lily's blood boiled. She wasn't sure what to do or say next. She snarled her lip.

Finn opened his eyes and lifted his head. "You know what? I can hitchhike from here." He stepped out of the carriage and almost bumped into Lily. He turned back and pointed at her. "I'll be happy if our paths *never* cross again!"

Lily's heart pounded in her ears. Why was he so mean? As he walked away, she wanted to tell him he's the weirdo. But as much as she wanted to blurt that, she held her tongue, especially with her friends listening nearby.

She had to say something, though. Lily pointed a finger back at Finn and spit out words.

"How quickly you forgot Briella flew!"

Finn turned back, his color pale.

Chapter Seven

To Help Me

Lily clenched her jaw as Finn flagged down a man driving a horse-drawn wagon. After a nod from the driver, he wedged himself between two bundles on the rear tailgate. Even though it wasn't terribly kind of her, Lily was glad he wasn't with them anymore. Finn wiggled his fingers at Lily with a sly smile on his face as the wagon drove away. She wanted to wiggle her fingers back like he did but kept them bunched in a fist. She had done all she could with friendly and gracious ways.

Mary and the others stood in a field of grass. "Lily, Come on!" Mary called. Lily ran to catch up.

Lily and her friends fanned out across the field. As she picked her steps through the hay, she felt like she was part of an undefeated soccer team, sure they could win against any opponent.

Descending down a bank to a small beach on Gala Lake, the group came upon two men standing waist-high in the water. One man had his head bowed and hands cupped in front of him while the other, wearing an orange shirt, had a hand on his shoulder. He gently lowered the reverent man into the water and then brought him back up. A baptism. The man who had gone under wiped his face.

Briella stepped forward under swooping butterflies. "Greetings, Philip." She nodded to the other man. "And to you, kind sir."

"Greetings," said Philip. "You must be Briella the White with all those butterflies."

"I am, and these are my friends."

As Philip and the man walked to the beach, Hannah asked, "My dear young man, are you even twenty?"

"All of nineteen, ma'am," said Philip, the sun settling on his orange shirt.

Hannah grinned from ear to ear. "What a sweet young man you are! And who is this with you?"

"This is Eth who wished to be baptized immediately."

Lily scrunched her eyebrows. Eth's ears did not stick out like everyone else's but were flush against his head. They looked slightly mangled. *Had they been cropped at one time?*

"There is no time like the present," said Paul, shaking his hand.

Eth agreed, shook Paul's hand, and then faced Philip. "Thank you for taking the time to explain the Old Text to me. I will never forget your gentleness."

"Peace to you," said Philip.

Eth bowed to everyone and walked toward Bethem, his shirt and pants soaking wet.

Bluey fluttered over Briella. "Your gentle spirit during these last days strengthens us."

Philip held out a hand for Bluey to land as he looked toward the dark sky beyond the mountain. "We cannot let dark skies prevent us from carrying on."

"That is correct." Briella grew brighter. "We have great news: Elstar has appeared!"

Philip stepped back and his eyes shone brilliantly while Bluey flew over his head. "This is indeed great news!" His smile revealed dazzling white teeth.

Bluey flew back to Briella. "Will you journey with us?"

"Of course! To the very end."

His smile rested on Lily, whose face turned warm when she realized she had been vibrantly smiling back at him.

***

Philip sat where Finn had sat in the carriage. His pleasant voice resonated in Lily's ears as he explained how Eth had once had his ears cropped, just as Lily suspected.

Lily's face twisted in anguish. "That must have hurt."

"I'm sure it did," said Philip. "But he's a changed man. He wanted to declare his identification as an Elstarian by being baptized as the Old Text says to."

The baptismal tank in church came to Lily's mind. She had stood in the water with the pastor and made her declaration. She knew baptism was an outward sign of an inward decision to be a follower of Jesus Christ, God's anointed.

As the two horse-drawn open carriages rolled along on a country road, they passed through a grove of pine trees. Something caught Lily's attention and she peered into the trees at objects running parallel to them.

"What are those?" she asked, pointing. "Elephants?"

The ground shook and jiggled the carriage.

Briella sprang up from her seat. "Stop the carriage!" The driver pulled back hard on the reins and the horses stepped sideways.

Branches flew like sparks as a pack of twenty or more huge coyotes plowed through the pine grove and changed direction, shoving up against trees and scraping bark as they charged toward the carriages. Appalled, Lily's body tightened and her fingers gripped the edge of the carriage.

The horses snorted and jerked as the large coyotes formed a circle around the carriages. Lily sunk in her seat, so did Mary, and the hair on her arms stood straight up. Her eyes opened wide as they fixed on the disfigured face of a coyote, slashes across its eyes. A muscular man with cropped ears on its back showed sharp teeth. The coyotes howled. They gnashed their teeth and dug their claws into the ground, tossing up patches of dirt.

"I am Region!" yelled the man on the lead coyote. The other men cheered. The coyotes paced, waiting to pounce. "You are not welcome here!"

A high-pitched yell triggered barks. Lily plugged her ears. Another coyote drew close and towered over the carriage. Lily clung to Mary and they both sunk further into the seat, closing their eyes. "Do something, Briella!"

Lily peeked to see Briella grab flowers from her pouch and throw them into the air. They transformed into lightning bolts and streaked high into the sky before falling and torpedoing into the coyotes and their riders. In an instant, all of them turned into stone statues except the leader and his coyote.

Growls and gnashes stopped. Lily swallowed what felt like sandpaper.

Region roared at his petrified pack and pounded his mount as hard as he could with his fist. "You will die! All of you! Sapphira's army will destroy you!" His coyote hissed and scooped dirt with its claw before turning back to the shadows of the pine grove.

Briella's butterflies flapped their wings as she picked another flower. She tossed the bloom that immediately transformed into a lightning streak. It chased Region like a persistent mosquito until the lightning caught him, changing him too, and the coyote, into a statute.

Lily's heart pounded in her chest. In the eerie quiet, she was sure her friends could hear it.

John placed a hand over his chest. "It's over now."

Philip let out a sigh. "Yes, it's over. They won't hurt us."

In the other carriage, Job clapped his hands. "Hooray! I said to myself, that's the way to do it!"

"Woo hoo!" yelled Hannah beside him.

"Is everyone all right over there?" asked Briella.

"Yes! We're all good," called Job.

Briella put her arms out as butterflies returned gracefully to her head and sleeves. "Let peace be upon you all." She resumed a poised sitting position.

"As it says in the Old Text," added Philip, sitting and smiling at Lily, "the way of the wicked will perish."

Lily looked up at a lifeless coyote peering down at her, its fixed pupils white stone.

Mary clutched her arm. "He can't hurt you."

"Not with Briella," said Lily, her confidence returning.

"Yes. But it's because you're the spirit seer. No one can hurt the spirit seer." Mary's encouraging look sent her words to Lily's heart where they could be treasured.

The driver wiped his brow with a handkerchief then snapped the reins. They meandered through the statues, Lily looking up at the creatures in their last moments.

***

Leaving the pine grove, the land opened to reveal the city of Jerul strategically placed on a hill with a commanding view of Gala Lake. The late afternoon sunshine shone on majestic buildings and reflected on scalloped rooftops. Lily loved how they sparkled like jewels. She scanned the rocking tops of ship's masts in Jerul's harbor and marveled at walls of white marble stretched around the fortified city.

Traffic increased on the road leading into the city's front gate. Lily loved the rows of colorful flowers that stretched for thousands of feet on both sides of the entrance. The foot-thick marble walls supported a massive stone archway. Vines hung down and tickled her face as they passed through the gate.

Inside, a crowd of people gathered at a fish market where a man hollered prices and people handed him money for their purchases. People reclined at tables in front of cafés sipping drinks under balconies decorated with flowers.

"The king and queen will be expecting us," Briella ran her fingers across the wood frame of the carriage, a look of concern flooding her face, "... provided Pity-Petty was successful with his flight."

Lily swiped overspray from her face from a water fountain while Mary took a corner piece of her poncho and wiped her cheek. "I'm sure he was," said Lily. Behind the fountain, bushes sculpted in the shape of elephants, camels, and birds lined a pool.

A stark and angular building loomed before them with red flags flapping in the breeze. The image of a white crown with pointy teeth on each flag grabbed Lily's attention. She stared at the words "Temple of the Cropped Ears" in red letters below the steeple. The booming voice of a man in a red robe and matching headpiece soared above a crowd gathered on the front steps.

Mary whispered, "What's going on here?"

Paul grew quiet. "That's a priest. It looks like he's about to perform the independence ceremony. I've tried to talk with these people but they won't listen to me."

Beside the priest, a young woman in a red gown held her head forward, her lamblike ears protruding. A red-hooded man stood on the other side wielding a knife.

"In recognition of your Elstarian independence, I hereby do crop thy ears!" The priest nodded to the hooded man and he carved into the woman's ears as she screamed.

Lily covered her mouth. Tears welled in her eyes as she watched blood flow down the sides of the woman's head. A man rushed forward with a red-hot iron rod and touched her ears as she screamed again. Then, a woman brought towels and held them to the sides of her head while the crowd cheered.

John's face contorted with pain.

Fighting back tears, Lily locked eyes with the priest as they rolled past. She heard whispers in the crowd and caught strange stares. When a man popped out of the crowd and tried to blend in beside the carriage, matching its pace, Lily froze. He ducked then looked around.

"Finn!"

"Shh!" Finn held a bag close to his chest and tossed it under the bench in the carriage. He glanced at Lily then took off running, zigzagging between people in the crowd. A police officer on horseback chased him down. People opened a path to let the officer pursue Finn who ran headlong into two other policemen waiting ahead. They snatched his arms and held him in place.

"Frisk him!" demanded the officer, dismounting.

Finn shot an angry look at Lily. They checked his pockets. Looking confused, they said to the officer, "Nothing."

The officer's eyes bulged. "Search that carriage!"

After Lily and her friends quickly exited the carriage, the officer found the bag and held it up. "Whose is this?" He opened it and took out wallets, loose money, and jewelry. "We've caught our pickpocket." He stepped down from the carriage and eyed Finn. "Take him to the station."

Finn tossed his hands up. "Wait!" He pointed at Lily. "They told me to do it. I'm just their gopher."

Lily gawped. "Don't be ridiculous, Finn!"

"See!" said Finn. "How does she know my name? And look at her ears!"

Lily glanced left and right without moving her head. The officer stepped closer to inspect her ears.

"Interesting," said the officer. "All of you will go to the station."

"Sir, they are innocent. I can assure you," said Joseph, who approached the officer.

"Then they'll have nothing to worry about."

Mary patted Lily's tense shoulder. "This will be straightened out."

Just then, an old man holding the arm of an old woman came up to Briella. "Excuse us. Are you Briella the White?"

"Yes."

"Then, have the eagles flown?"

"They have."

The man smiled. "And the lamb has appeared? Is this correct?"

Briella nodded. "Yes."

106

The old man's eyes danced. He turned to his wife and spoke as loud as his frail voice would allow him. "Miriam, did you hear that? Elstar has appeared!"

Chapter Eight

Face Every Trial

The long squeal of a jail door opening rang down the dank corridor of a dark prison lit only by torches. Shabby cots stacked one above the other were the only furniture in the dingy stone cell. The guard stepped aside to let Lily enter. She hesitated at the door, shooting an angry look at Finn in the adjacent cell where he and the men had already entered. In the oppressive air, she stepped over the threshold, turning to see the guard pull the door shut with a clang. Walls of stone upon stone formed the tomblike cell. No air circulated in the sealed confinement, and the lack of a window gave no hope for that to change.

"We need to make sure you are not in cahoots with this man, Finn," said the sheriff. "We'll get to the bottom of this." He left the attending guard at a desk in charge after telling him about a riot occurring in the city.

A rat scuttled in front of Lily's foot. "Ewww!" She stumbled backward then scrambled to the cot and lifted her feet off the ground.

Mary joined her, her feet up too.

"I hate rats!" said Lily.

The rodent ripped along ragged rocks until it ran out of sight. "It's gone now," said Mary, patting Lily's shoulder. She pulled the purple ribbon from her hair and let her locks fall around her ears. "I'm sorry for this."

Lily clutched her legs at the shins, wedging her heels on the frame of the cot. "It's not your fault." Through steel bars, she glared at Finn sitting on a cot.

It's his fault. Look at him over there. We're in jail because of him. I would never do anything to end up in jail.

Finn bent over with his elbows on his knees and his face in his hands.

I hope he's sorry. He should be.

John rested his arms through the cell bars facing the women. "How hopeless that young woman must have been to go to the extent of having her ears cut off. I wish she would accept her creator's love for her."

Deborah paced along the bars separating the two cells. She had insisted on being put in jail even though she was in the other carriage. "Many have little peace, but remain strong. And I'm sure our friends have gone to get help."

109

Paul sat further down the cot from Finn. "We know that the Old Text warns of these faithless times and times of lawlessness."

Finn dropped his hands from his face. "Pfft! The Old Text? That's just gibberish writings of weak-minded men!" Finn covered his face with his hands again.

What an idiot! No. I don't think he's sorry.

Philip walked around the men's cell talking with his hands. "The priests are a brood of vipers living for their own truth. They are ruthless. There is nothing gentle in their ways."

"Evil is prevalent but do not give up,' said Briella, her butterflies motionless in the dead air. "Truth cannot be altered no matter what."

Lily found comfort in her friend's words. Even so, she couldn't help but wonder if she should have gone home. Was her father back with pizza by now? To be home would be way better than the gloomy place she was in now.

Mary touched her arm. "The journey will end well. It's best to take our minds off this bit of gloom. We can focus on things we are thankful for." Mary's smile drew a small one from Lily. "I'm thankful for sunshine, apple trees, birds and puppies, the blue sky, and the blue ocean, and waves— especially those that look like white foamy running horses, which I'd like to paint."

Lily faced Mary. "You paint?"

Mary nodded. "I want to be an artist."

Lily's face brightened. "What kind of paints do you use?"

"Oils. But I'm not very good."

Lily could hardly believe that. "I bet you are."

110

"I'm trying. Now, you name things you are thankful for."

Lily grew quiet. She shot another angry look at Finn and said dryly, "Freedom."

Mary looked down. "Me too."

No one spoke for a while until Deborah started humming a tune that weaved around the heavy air and into Lily's ears.

"That's "Amazing Grace," said Lily, glad she knew it.

Deborah stopped humming. "Would you sing it?"

"No, I think you should sing it," replied Lily, not wanting to sing a solo.

Deborah looked at Lily confused. "I would but that's not the name of *my* song."

A wrinkle formed on Lily's brow. She had been sure that was the song.

"The name of my song is "Peace over Faithful Mountain.""

Mary looked at Lily and then Deborah. "Why don't you sing your song and then you sing yours?"

Lily rubbed the back of her neck while peering into Mary's eyes. *Here? In Jail?*

Mary raised her eyebrows and flipped her hands open. "There isn't anything else to do."

A warm flush filled Lily's cheeks, embarrassed again to be the center of attention. But maybe it was vain of her to think that. She did have a problem with being shy. She closed her eyes and imagined herself sitting next to Ada in church. She took a deep breath.

Amazing grace, how sweet the sound that saved a wretch like me...

Lily focused on pitch and intonation like any good musician would.

I once was lost, but now am found, was blind, but now I see.

Lily held the last note extra long, letting her tone fill the dark cracks between the stones. When the sound faded away, she felt Mary's touch on her elbow. Lily faced Mary with a smile but Mary was crying. Her tears made Lily's eyes grow misty.

"Exquisite!" said Deborah. "I was transported out of this dreary place."

Mary sniffled and wiped her eyes with her poncho. "You have a good heart. That's why you sing so well."

Lily knew better about the good heart. It wasn't as good as Mary thought.

"What do the words mean to you, Lily?" asked John.

Lily blinked and turned her head toward John. She thought about the lyrics and formed her answers.

"**Amazing grace**—because grace is amazing." Lily chuckled and made a silly face.

"**How sweet the sound**—grace must be a sweet sound!" Lily nodded at Mary, who was no longer crying and smiled at her answer.

"**That saved a wretch like me.**" *That saved a wretch like me.* Lily bit her lip before looking back at John. "Wretch?" She looked at the prison floor. "I'm not sure what 'wretch' means." She remembered a word from a cartoon then lifted her head and glared at Finn. "I think it means someone who is despicable."

Briella strolled beside the prison bars while Bluey swooped in between them. "Synonyms for the word 'wretch' include scoundrel, villain, criminal, good-for-nothing, creep, rat, snake-in-the-grass, lowlife, toe rag, and varlet." She stopped and raised her eyebrows at Lily.

Lily looked down again. *But I'm not any of those things.*

"But even though you were once lost, you are now found?" asked Mary.

Mary's brown eyes peered into Lily's.

"And you were once blind, but now you see?"

All Lily could do was nod.

"And even deaf, but now you hear?" asked John.

Lily bit her lip again. *Am I despicable? I certainly would be if it weren't for the fact that Jesus died for my sins. Actually, I still am. But I'm saved.* Lily nodded to John as her understanding of grace increased.

Mary beamed. "Thank you for sharing your song. You sang beautifully. I wish I had your voice."

Repeated notes of trumpets blared outside the jail preventing Deborah from singing her song. The guard at the desk pushed his chair back, opened the door, and stepped back as the queen entered. He quickly bowed. "Your Majesty!"

The queen's golden dress glittered in the evening ray coming through the door and a golden tiara sparkled with jewels balanced atop her lamblike ears and golden afro-like hair. A blue diamond hung on a gold necklace and an indigo shawl wrapped around her shoulders. "Good evening," her clear voice penetrated the air.

"How may I serve thee, Queen Esther?" asked the guard.

"Release the prisoners, except for the one called Finn. He may serve out his time."

Lily and Mary jumped off the cot when the guard turned the key to unlock the doors of the cells. They joined the men to meet the queen.

But when Lily saw Finn sitting alone in the cell, slumped on the edge of the cot, she stopped and approached and touched her forehead to the bars, her head heavy and her mind searching for something to say.

114

Finn raised his head and stared at her. "So you're a wretch like me."

The heavy weight of Lily's head pressed against the bars. She wanted to lift it up and put distance between her and him but what kept her head glued to the bars was that Finn was right. She had not thought of herself as a wretch and without God, she would be.

There was nothing she could do. Lily pushed her head off the bars. "I hope you get out of here soon."

"Me too." Finn's empty stare fell to his hands.

His sad look tugged at Lily's heart. Had she followed the way of love when she wished him the same that he wished her? His lousiness for her lousiness? She took another look at Finn. *I am a work-in-progress. If there were more time, maybe I could do better. Maybe I could help him.* But there was no more time and her friends waited.

Briella's butterflies flapped their wings above the queen.

"Briella the White," said the queen with open arms, "Welcome! I am thrilled! A little bird gave me the most wonderful message."

Briella's eyes danced as the corners of her mouth lifted. "Pity-Petty. How is he?"

"He is well. He has been enjoying red grapes."

Briella grinned. "I do hope he has exercised moderation."

"He has. He is outside waiting for you." The queen turned to Lily. "Welcome to the royal city of Jerul, seer of the lamb."

Lily's skin tingled as she struggled for the right words. "Your Majesty." She lowered her head and curtsied deeply.

"Come. We will go to the palace now." Queen Esther strolled out of the jail.

Amidst a royal entourage, Hannah, Job, and Joseph ran to Lily and her friends and Pity-Petty flew to Briella's outstretched hand.

***

Pulled by a team of horses, the queen's royal carriage rolled along a pavement lined with balsam trees surrounding a large oval-shaped courtyard in front of a blue marble palace. Lily touched the plush material by the window. She could smell the fragrant balsam trees coming through the window.

Queen Esther smiled at Lily then spoke to Philip. "I am glad to meet you, Philip," said Queen Esther. "I have heard of you and your wonderful understanding of the Old Text."

"Thank you, Your Majesty."

"Tell me a favorite verse," said the queen.

Philip's eyes grew wide as he thought. "I am fond of the verse about how the price for salvation has been made."

The queen nodded. "One of my favorites as well." Then she looked out the window of the carriage.

When they pulled up to the grand entrance, an old gnarly tree caught Lily's attention. The stark, weathered bark curled up the trunk and no greenery adorned ugly, twisted branches. *I would think a grand palace like this would have a better tree than that.*

Under banners waving in the breeze, Pity-Petty lifted his head from Briella's lap when the carriage came to a stop. A guard flipped down the footstep.

John walked on the sidewalk from another carriage to the tree. "The white tree! It's been such a long time since I last looked on it."

"The crowning day is coming," said Queen Esther. "Welcome, my friends! We will freshen up for dinner and my servants will attend you."

Deborah smoothed out wrinkles in her blue coat. "I would not be opposed to freshening up."

The grand foyer led to a long hallway adorned with large windows and potted trees. Lily imagined herself as a princess, walking with the royal party.

Down the hallway, the queen stopped and addressed the men as a manservant opened a door. "Make yourselves comfortable and we will feast at seven o'clock." John, Job, Joseph, Paul, and Philip entered after each giving an appreciative nod to the queen.

Further down the hallway, a maidservant opened a different door.

"Prepare for dinner," said the queen. "Choose any outfit you wish." As Lily turned to enter, she watched Queen Esther stroll with Briella, Pity-Petty flying close and landing on branches of potted trees in the hallway. She wondered what they were talking about.

"Help yourselves to juice and crackers," said the maidservant. "There are four bedrooms connected to this main room. Each bedroom has a bath, soap, and towels. Choose an outfit from the rack by the sofa. Let me know if you need anything. I'll be outside the door."

Mary went directly to the table and poured juice into four cups. "Tea, anyone?" She laughed and then sampled a cracker.

"I'll have some," said Lily. "Thank you."

Hannah selected a dress from the rack and held it up to Mary. "Look at this purple satin dress. What do you think?"

Mary pointed with a half-eaten cracker, and then to the row of shoes beneath the rack. "I like that. And those matching velvety shoes!" She threw the rest of the cracker in her mouth and sprang up to pick up the shoes. "They're even my size!"

"That Queen Esther knows a thing or two," said Hannah. "I'm fond of this yellow blazer with matching skirt. Don't eat too much. You'll spoil your dinner." Hannah entered a bedroom.

Lily ate a cracker and then searched through the dresses, pulling out a green and gold one.

"Here are some gold-colored shoes," said Deborah. "Do you think you would be able to walk in these high heels?"

"I could," said Lily.

Deborah held up a blue crepe dress and gave Lily a grin before whisking into a room. Lily and Mary each took their dresses and entered their rooms.

The smell of lavender greeted Lily. A large poster bed filled the room with a free-standing bathtub in front of a fire blazing in the fireplace. Lily laid her dress on the bed and then stirred the water in the tub.

Perfect temperature.

After shedding her soiled traveling clothes, she eased into the warm water and the memory of the horrific attack on Gala

Lake dissipated with the warmth and fragrance engulfing her. She recalled Briella's words of peace amidst the attack of huge coyotes and sighed relief.

This is noble and fair and good and pleasant. She moved the fragrant water with her hand, glad for the freedom of the dingy jail. *And this is what any good princess would think upon.*

***

White flags with the image of a red Gambrel flanked each side of the double doors of the Great Hall. Over the doors, another design drew Lily's eyes. It was the same design as on the two narrow stones she had passed through when she first came into the world of Whule—a circle with two triangles, one on each side, and nine lines shooting out around the design.

"My!" said Hannah to the men. "Don't you all look handsome!"

Job adjusted his tie. "Thank you, and you all look exquisite!"

A palace guard opened the doors for Lily and her friends. Job extended his arm to Hannah. "Shall we?"

Joseph offered an arm to Deborah and she took it with a nod.

"Mary," said Paul, "may I have the honor?"

"Of course," said Mary.

Philip bowed to Lily. "I would be honored if you—the one with the glorious voice—would allow me to be your escort."

Lily blushed and took his arm.

John came alongside her. "I hope you don't mind me on your other arm!"

They laughed together then strolled into the Great Hall. The last of the day's sunshine streamed through tall stained-glass windows along the right side of the Great Hall and across the marble floor to the other side. Violin and flute music grew louder as they made their way through the stately hall.

John's rich voice resonated over the marble floors. "What a beautiful place! What beautiful windows!"

At the entrance to a private dining room, a small music ensemble was gathered. Lily didn't know the tune they were playing but could tell it was a waltz. The musicians played softly as Queen Esther welcomed everyone. Pity-Petty wore his purple hat and fluffed his feathers while firmly fixed on Briella's uplifted hand.

Only one table occupied the dining room under a chandelier of candles. Pity-Petty flew to a fancy bird stand beside an elaborate stained-glass window while butterflies swooped under the chandelier and over dome-covered plates. Waiters pulled out chairs and Lily took her seat.

Rich colors of gold, green, blue, and purple reflected on stained-glass windows and danced in Lily's eyes. The scene in the center window featured a man holding a lamb under an indigo-colored sky. The window to the left pictured sheep among lilies on a hillside with the Gambrel on the horizon. The right window displayed an empty tomb with long-eared people sitting at long tables, feasting in a yellow field. Peace filled Lily's heart. The images looked very similar to the windows in her church.

With the candlelight gleaming on her blue diamond necklace, Queen Esther addressed everyone. "With great joy, I received the message from Briella the White. How long we have waited for such a time as this!" She paused to smile at each person around the table but then frowned. "I am sorry you will miss the king. He was called away to the city of Cush. I have already sent word to him of the lamb's appearance and he will be overjoyed to hear this news. Now, may you enjoy tonight's meal served in your honor."

Lily bowed her head as the queen prayed for courage and self control. When she finished, 'amens' sounded around the table.

The waiters lifted the dome coverings over their plates and Job licked his lips. "Bell tinger soup!"

Lily dipped her soup spoon into the broth, realizing how hungry she was. The savory liquid tasted like chicken with a hint of red bell pepper.

The waiters held platters and made their way around the table. Lily scooped a large spoonful of mashed potatoes on her plate. She made a well in her spuds and filled it with gravy. She selected meat and added butter to peas. Then a waiter offered a baked dish she didn't recognize. She hesitated.

"That's a puffy cheese soufflé. It's good!" said Philip.

Lily accepted a portion, and from another platter, shoveled corn and salad on her plate.

"Leave room for chocolate waddle cake!" Job pointed to the dessert table full of pies, cakes, assorted fruit, and a tall chocolate cake that leaned slightly to the side.

Lily dabbed the sides of her mouth with a napkin. "I will."

Briella stood, her butterflies resting on their places on her head and belled sleeves. "Tonight, we celebrate the nine fruits. No weapon formed against this council shall prosper."

***

After dinner, Lily returned to the royal bedroom and dressed in a satiny nightgown that had been laid out for her on the poster bed. She found a porcelain bowl beside the bed filled with white rose petals and couldn't resist plunging her hand into the bowl, feeling the silky smooth petals against her hand. She selected one and pulled the velvety flower piece through her fingers while gazing at the fire still burning in the fireplace.

Amazing grace that saved a wretch like me. Why am I of extreme importance? I struggle to be gracious to someone who isn't gracious to me.

She let the petal fall back into the bowl.

Incredibly tired, Lily pulled the curtains closed on the poster bed but kept the foot of the bed opened to watch the fire. Then, like a true daughter of the King, she lay down near rose petals, sweet, soft, and luxurious, and prayed for Finn's salvation before falling fast asleep.

Chapter Nine

Relying on Prayer

Roar!

In the dark, early hours, Lily frantically clutched the bed covers close to her chin. Every muscle tightened in her body. She darted her eyes back and forth in the enclosed curtains of the poster bed.

Roar!

Lily tossed the blanket over her head. *What was that? A grizzly bear? Another distorted coyote?*

A rapid knock at the door made her hold her breath.

"Lily? Are you awake? It's Deborah. Can I come in?"

"Yes." Lily peeked out from beneath the blanket as Deborah hurried in. "Did you hear that?"

Deborah crouched. "I sure did. Something awful must have made that sound. We're going to see what it is. Do you want to come with us?"

Not wanting to be left alone, Lily scrambled out of bed and donned her robe. She and Deborah met Hannah and Mary in the gathering room with moonlight shining through a window onto their frightened faces. Deborah snuck to the door to the hallway then sprang back when she opened it. In the light of flickering candles, Pity-Petty had flown by. Deborah ran after him, Lily, Mary, and Hannah on her heels.

When they reached the palace foyer, Lily flinched as flashes of light lit up large windows, one of which Briella and John peered through. Job and the others hunched down, gawking out a different window. Guards gripped swords and tightened their grasp on daggers they held in their hands. Little Pity-Petty landed on an indoor tree by the door.

Lily crept to the window with the women and the hair on her neck stood up. A large reptile creature with red wings and red eyes swished its spiked tail and stomped on the ground. Its beastly rider, also with red eyes and wearing a metal crown, cracked a whip, splicing the night air with streaks of white light.

Briella turned around, her face as white as her hair. "I cannot stop this creature but perhaps I can wound it." She snatched flowers from her pouch and took a deep breath. After a nod to the head guard to open the door, Briella ran out but Pity-Petty jumped off the tree and flew out before her.

"No, Pity-Petty! Stop!" The royal carrier pigeon darted and swooped, distracting the hideous beast mounted on the back of the scaly, red-winged dragon.

Crack!

The beast had snapped his whip again.

"Briella the White, you cannot destroy me," the beast bellowed in a long tone.

Lily clenched the window sill when the dragon's tail demolished a water fountain. Then the beast turned the dragon to face the old gnarly tree. At the rider's raspy yell, the dragon opened its mouth, let out a loud screech, and torched the old gnarly white tree with a stream of fire. The beast laughed and turned the dragon back around.

"I am Sayta the Formidable. Today, you will all die a gruesome death! And Sapph, my pet, will eat your remains."

Crack!

Briella planted her feet firmly. Her butterflies lifted strands of her long white hair as she heaved handfuls of flowers that transformed into lightning bolts as soon as they left her hand. With all her strength, she heaved her weapons, most bouncing off the dragon's tough skin, until one found its way in. Sapph reared and Sayta fell backward off the dragon.

As Sayta scrambled to his feet, Sapph let out a cry from a fire burning in his side. He shook his scaly frame and opened his mouth to torch Briella. Pity-Petty dashed in front of the dragon's eyes, giving Briella time to throw another lightning bolt which sank deep into his belly. Sapph squealed as fire spread throughout his body. His scaled turned red before he turned into a massive flame and then disintegrated into ash.

125

Briella swatted her hand. "Get out of the way, Pity-Petty!"

Sayta the Formidable roared at the ruin of Sapph. He swung his arm and hit Pity-Petty with a powerful blow. It sent the pigeon's purple hat propelling and his body smashing into the trunk of a balsam tree.

"No!" Briella wailed. She threw more lightning bolts at Sayta.

As Sayta continued to roar, the guards mustered strength and organized a line of attack in front of the palace.

"It's useless, Briella," Sayta yelled. "You cannot kill me. No one here can." His voice trailed into the black night.

But in the dark, Elstar appeared between him and the white tree still burning, his body glowing. He stomped a front foot.

Sayta turned around as a lightning bolt hit him in the back of the head. He raised his arm to snap the whip but the fire on the old gnarly tree miraculously jumped off and onto him, igniting his head. Flames spread from his head to his feet. He wobbled, then the all-consuming fire reduced him to ash. Only a charred spot remained on the walkway next to the other charred spot from Sapph.

Lily forced a swallow in the eerie quiet that followed. As a lightning bolt sizzled and faded away, her friends inched toward Briella.

"You did it, Briella!" exclaimed Mary.

Briella bent over. "No. I did not."

Lily beamed. "It was Elstar. Didn't you see him?"

John's ears sprang up. "That would explain it. Only Elstar could destroy such an evil creature from the Abyss."

Briella stood. "That is true. Praise to Elstar! He has saved us!"

Then she ran to Pity-Petty and stopped in the grass. At the base of the balsam tree, she picked up his lifeless body. Her voice cracked as she cradled his body in her hands. "Pity-Petty. Oh, Pity-Petty."

In the still hours of the early morning, Pity-Petty's body was laid to rest in a small box covered with a purple blanket. Queen Esther gently took the box from Briella's hands and placed it on her throne.

Under a dark sky, Finn stopped running in the middle of the road and faced his portly friend. "Did you hear that?"

Buzz pointed to a red blaze in the night sky over the blue marble palace. "Dang! What in tarnation? Did you see that? The whole sky lit up!"

Finn gawked at flashes of light streaking across the night sky. His body froze. Too many weird things had been happening. He made a quick decision. "We're checking that out."

The two men ran toward the palace. Buzz's heavy weight pounded the pavement as he ran.

"By the way, thanks for making bail for me," said Finn as he ran beside his friend. "I owe you, bud."

"No prob. Heck, you always owe me!"

Finn outran Buzz and arrived at the palace first. He pulled back a balsam branch. A chill skidded down his back as he watched a beast mounted on the back of a dragon with red wings and spiked tail crack a whip, igniting sparks. His heart pounded when the dragon breathed fire on the old gnarly tree. And his mind raced when the fire on the tree jumped back on the beast.

***

Butterflies huddled close to Briella's sad face, their heads drooping. The brown butterflies closed their wings and looked like dead leaves. As a yellow flier made space, Lily placed a hand on Briella's shoulder. "I'm sorry, Briella."

Briella patted Lily's hand. "Thank you. I know I should not be this downcast. He was just a bird." Briella wiped a tear. "But he was also a longtime friend."

Mary's face brightened. "You will see him again."

Briella nodded. She stood from a fancy chair in the throne room and walked to a podium, her butterflies trailing behind her and then landing on their usual places. A large book lay open on the podium and Briella ran her hand across the smooth pages of the book.

"A prophecy was fulfilled this morning. The Old Text says: 'No morning light will greet Sapph, the iron-scaled dragon, who will carry his rider to Sapphira the Sorceress to answer a summons. Allowed to be conjured in the depths of Whule beneath the Gambrel, Sayta the Formidable will never see the light of day.' "

The serious tone in Briella's voice brought silence from everyone. Lily's breathing grew shallow in the hushed moment until steps across the marble floor in the Great Hall startled her. Her eyes darted to a servant carrying a small dish, his steps quickening on his way to the queen.

Queen Esther scanned the report and her body trembled. She rose from her chair and staggered to a stained-glass window, gripping the woodwork edge. "What grave news! The king and those with him have been captured. Oh, my poor husband! Briella, please read the prophecy of the Feast of the Nine Fruits. I have always been comforted by it."

Briella located the passage in the book and spoke in an expressive voice, trying to cheer up the queen. "On that new day, at early dawn, light will span across the sky. The new land will be formed and the faithful remnant will dine with Elstar at the Feast of the Nine Fruits. And the seer from the other world will bear witness so she might grow ears of wisdom."

Lily met Briella's gaze.

Mary nudged Lily. "What do you think of those words?"

Lily had been too busy thinking to catch Mary's question. Her heart beat faster. "What?"

"The prophecy. What do you think about the prophecy?"

Lily looked into Mary's eyes. "I can't believe I'm part of a prophecy."

"Well, I think you are."

The upward turn at the corners of Mary's smile reminded Lily of her mother—the smile that everything would work out fine. God was always in control. Somehow, He was allowing this journey.

Lily glanced at everyone in the throne room. "As long as I travel with all of you, I'm willing to journey to the end."

Queen Esther took a deep breath then let it out. "It is not far. We must maintain our self-control. Get ready for today. Then meet me in the garden where we will pray."

***

The morning sunshine streaked through trees in the palace garden where Lily gathered with her friends in front of a chapel. She wore her traveling clothes again, which had been washed and dried.

Queen Esther wore an indigo-colored gown with matching shawl. Her tiara crowned her full head of hair, resting on her lamblike ears, and the blue diamond necklace graced her neck.

130

"Find quiet places to pray. We will begin this day right. And, I decree no food with be eaten until we see Elstar face to face." With John and Hannah, she entered the chapel.

Deborah and Job settled into a quiet decorative alcove featuring a blue and brown mosaic of a gambrel. Joseph and Paul sat at opposite ends of a pool teeming with fish, pink flowers overhanging from lush green foliage. Philip knelt under a willow tree near orange blossoms while Briella stood by, always watching.

Mary turned to Lily. "Where do you want to pray?"

Lily shrugged.

Mary looked down a path. "Let's walk there."

Down a lane, Lily spotted a purple flowering tulip tree. "My grandparents have that kind of tree."

"Let's pray there then," said Mary, leading the way. They sat in the grass beneath the tree. Mary ran her hand over the tops of the blades of grass. "I love our creation. There is so much beauty. And I loved how Briella said no weapon formed against us shall prosper."

Lily studied the intricate blossoms. "What does that mean?"

"It means we'll win!" Mary laughed but then grew serious. "It means there is a powerful force that protects us and guides and corrects and even gives us comfort." Mary lifted her palms in the air and looked up. "It comes from the creator." Mary then folded her hands and bowed her head.

Lily turned around to give Mary privacy and looked across the garden.

Is she talking about the Holy Spirit? Am I the one to make a difference in Finn's life? But I'm no good, God. Why would you want me? I can't be of great importance. Oh. Yes. I remember. I prayed on Peaceful Rock, asking for help.

Lily liked praying with Mary nearby. Actually, with all of her friends. She shared a oneness in their point of view. That wasn't always the case back home.

She recalled a time when she silently prayed before eating her lunch in the school cafeteria. When she had finished, a classmate snickered at her and said that the food wasn't getting any better by staring at it. Lily had let that bother her, even though the classmate didn't know that she had been.

Lily quieted herself and bowed her head, comfortable to call on God.

Dear Heavenly Father, I know You're watching over me and that You love me. I'm sorry I haven't been the best Christian. Help me to follow You better. In Jesus' name, Amen.

Wooly fur rubbed up against her arm and she opened her eyes. "Elstar!"

He lay down and Lily sunk her fingers into the soft fleece at the back of his neck. She looked over his body for burn marks but there weren't any before cradling his head in her hands and peering into his warm brown eyes. "You are powerful—more powerful than you look. Of course you're not going to be burnt!"

"Who are you talking to?" asked Mary, her eyes wide and her face beaming.

Lily glanced back at Elstar. "Can't you see him?"

"No. I wish I could. I'm thrilled he's right there! But it's okay that I can't see him. I will soon. I know he's there, as you say. I don't need to see him to know that."

Elstar head-butted Lily's arm then turned his head toward a small apple orchard. Lily turned as well to see two men making their way through the grove. One was large and lumbered along and the other walked with a familiar, sauntering gait. Finn.

With each step they made, Lily's heart panged out another beat. Her stomach churned with the thought of facing Finn again but Elstar pressed his chin hard into her arm.

Okay. I'm focused.

Finn and his friend came under the tulip tree. "So, we meet again. I made bail, thanks to my good friend Buzz here." He motioned with his head as he sat on the ground.

Buzz plopped down beside him, his large ears flopping. "And my good friend Finn here is going to pay me back, not to mention what you owe that jack wagon over in Nain."

"Don't bring him up. I'll pay him." Finn replied to Buzz.

Pointing at Lily's ears, Buzz laughed. "Shoot!" What happened to you, little girl?"

Finn snapped. "I told you her ears were different."

Buzz snorted and then grimaced. "Well, I wasn't expecting that!"

Lily squared her jaw, thinking that Buzz could take a long walk on a short pier as far as she was concerned. But Elstar nuzzled his nose in her elbow. A Sunday School teacher entered her mind who had said, *"When I get to Heaven, I want to*

133

hear *'Well done, my good and faithful servant."* Lily had decided she wanted to hear that too. And even now.

Finn gave Buzz a stern look. "Why don't you pipe down."

"So-rry." Buzz looked disgusted then stretched out on his back, looking up at the sky.

Finn eyed Lily. "So, what happened this morning?"

Lily glanced at Buzz and then back at Finn. "You saw that?"

"*I* didn't see anything except a red sky," Buzz cut in.

Finn snapped at Buzz again. "*I* saw it! I saw it clear as day."

Finn waited for an answer. Lily hesitated then picked a blade of grass. "I don't know. It was a pretty scary creature. Maybe your world is coming to an end."

Finn's stare made Lily's heart race. She didn't want to talk about the end times but the words had already left her mouth.

"The world can't be coming to an end," said Finn.

Lily looked at Mary, wondering what to say. Elstar rubbed his head on her arm. His wooly touch calmed her. *I know of the powerful force. I've got to explain things slowly. And preferably in the kindest way possible.*

"In my world," Lily paused, "the Bible talks about an end time. God, who is my Creator, has written what's going to happen. If the Old Text is written by your creator, then maybe what's written is true."

Buzz sat up. "Now that's hogwash!"

Lily looked at Mary again with wide eyes and then clutched the back of Elstar's neck. Her face grew warm. She didn't want to get in an argument.

Mary look right at Buzz. "You shouldn't speak like that in front of Elstar."

Buzz spit on the ground. "Elstar? He doesn't even exist!"

"Yes he does," said Mary. "He's lying down right next to Lily."

Buzz squinted. He pointed to the space where Elstar rested. "Are you saying he's right *there*?"

Lily put her hand on Elstar's head. A centered calm continued to soothe her. "Yes."

Buzz rolled onto his back and laughed. "Oh boy, Finn! You got a real nut here! Can we get on with this? I'm getting hungry."

Finn glared at Buzz. "Cool your heels." He looked at Lily then pointed at the spot and spoke softer. "You're saying Elstar is right there?"

Lily nodded.

"Wow. And you followed him?"

"Yes."

"Into this world?"

Lily nodded.

Finn hesitated then pinned Lily with steady pupils. "Aren't you afraid to be in a new world?"

"Well ..." Lily looked at Mary and then back to Finn. "Maybe ... but, not really."

Finn picked a blade of grass. "What makes you so brave?"

Brave? Am I? I'm not brave.

The warmth of Elstar's fleece reached into Lily's heart. There was an answer, and she knew what it was. "I'm not brave but the One inside me is."

"Inside you?" Finn tore the blade and tossed it.

"Wherever I go, He's with me."

"Lily!" Briella's voice carried from the chapel over the garden.

"Mary!" called John, also from the chapel.

The morning sunlight slanted across the garden to the chapel. The sunray beamed on the queen's blue diamond necklace.

Buzz lowered his head and caught a reflection of the gem in his eye. "Looks like it's time to scram. Don't want to get caught on the palace grounds." He ducked. "Not with our track record." He studied the queen then scrambled to his feet, staying low to the ground as he snuck away to the apple orchard.

Finn crouched. "We didn't mean any harm here. Could you not tell anyone we were here?"

"Sure." Lily looked at Mary then back at Finn. "But if we're asked if you were here, we're not going to lie."

Finn locked eyes with Lily before sneaking away. "No. I wouldn't think you would."

Chapter Ten

Clothed and Ready

A trumpet fanfare blared over the palace garden. Lily analyzed the three notes she heard. They formed a major triad. Then, for almost a full minute, the trumpets played a tune similar to a hymn she knew—"Crown Him with Many Crowns". Lily, Mary, and Elstar listened to the trumpets until they stopped playing. Guards ran from the front of the palace to the queen.

Mary faced Lily and pulled at her arm. "Come on."

Lily ran with Mary, Elstar running beside them, until they reached the queen and the company of friends.

"Your Majesty!" the head guard called as he bowed. "The white tree. Come quickly!"

The queen motioned to Lily and Mary to hurry with her and the others to the front of the palace. They stopped in front of the old gnarly tree but it wasn't old and gnarly anymore. The white tree that had caught on fire and on which the fire had leapt off was now blooming with fragrant white blossoms and dark green leaves in the early morning sunlight.

Briella's butterflies landed on the branches while Bluey and the rest of her tiara flittered on her head. She declared in a singsong voice, "Here, the white tree has blossomed which means we have come to the last day!"

John clasped his hands. "Those who have ears to hear, let them hear! Hannah, do you have a copy of the Old Text?"

"Indeed I do."

"Let's hear the prophecy about today."

Hannah pulled the Old Text out of her bag. She opened the book toward the back and scanned with her finger before stopping. "Here it is. 'When the white tree blooms, Elstar will be fully known at the Gambrel at three o'clock that day.'" Hannah looked up from the book, her face aglow. "That is today!"

Paul beamed. "Let's go! If we leave now, we should arrive in time."

"Jolly good! Jolly good!" said Job. "We have waited long for this day."

138

Lily pointed to Elstar as the base of the tree. "Elstar is happy too. He's jumping up and down."

Queen Esther stared at the place Lily indicated.

"Don't you see him?" asked Lily.

The queen shook her head.

Lily looked into the eyes of her friends. "Can any of you see him?"

John placed a hand on her shoulder. "We don't need to see him to know he exists."

Queen Esther lifted her arms. "Elstar is here among us and his word comes to pass. Let us prepare for this last day with prayer and fasting."

Lily followed her friends into the palace, glancing back to see Briella's butterflies return to her sleeves and Elstar rest under the white tree.

***

In the coat room, Job tried on a coat. "This fits nicely over my tweed jacket. Going to be cold up there on Abar Mountain. Made of wool from the Highlands of Olan, you know. I said to myself, such a treat to obtain such fine clothing from that good place. Better make sure we're all suited up, but my jacket will do fine for now." Job removed the coat and placed it in the trunk with the other coats.

Deborah tried on a pair of mittens. "The Gosi Pass is narrow and the carriages won't get through. I imagine we'll each ride a horse."

The queen placed a finger to her chin. "We'll need eleven." She ordered servants to make preparations.

"Lanterns too," said John. "We'll go help put them on the horses." John left, Job and Joseph following.

Deborah stuffed mittens, hats, and scarves into Hannah's bag and then tucked them into the trunk. "I never thought I'd cross the Gosi Pass. Remember that children's rhyme? How did it go? 'You cross Gosi. You lose, you die?'"

Philip closed the trunk lid. "No, I thought it was: 'You cross Gosi. I'll take your eye!'"

Lily raised her eyebrows. *Is this really wise to be going to this place?*

"Well, whatever it was," said Paul motioning to Philip to lift the trunk, "we're crossing it."

"This should be interesting, right Lily?" asked Mary.

Lily's wide eyes indicated fright, a clear 'maybe not'.

"Courage," said Mary. "Remember, no harm will befall you, and this trip must be for your good."

***

Guards held the reins of horses lined in front of the palace, each with an unlit lantern hanging from a chest harness. Another guard held the bridles of a two-horse team that would pull an open carriage with the trunk full of coats affixed to the back and two horses tethered behind.

Yellow and gold bands streaked across the morning sky. Briella frowned at the sun hanging low in the sky. "Take note: the sun will stop climbing today into the sky."

"Are you ready?" Mary asked Lily.

Lily wasn't sure she was, especially since Mary asked. But she replied, "I think so."

Mary patted her arm. "We'll be right here with you. And Elstar goes with us. There's no reason to think we walk in darkness." She looked around. "Where is he?"

"Under the white tree. I think he's waiting for us."

Philip took the reins from a guard and handed them to Lily. "Then we best get going. Here's your horse—Victormane. He's a gentle stallion, which is rare."

The horse's black mane fell across a smooth black coat. Lily breathed in the smell of horse as she stroked the animal's powerful neck and took the rough leather cords in her hands.

"Victormane," she repeated as she touched the horse's soft nose then looked at Philip. "But, I've never ridden a horse before and there's no saddle."

"His withers are here and you can hold there as I boost you up onto his back." Philip leaned over and interlocked his fingers for her foot.

Lily pulled herself up. The powerful muscles on the back of Victormane made her hope he wouldn't take off running.

"Good," said Paul, on his horse. "Then just give a kick with your heels and off you go." He clicked his tongue and his horse walked forward.

Lily kicked and Victormane matched the walking pace.

"Now pull back on the reins to stop, like this," said Paul, demonstrating.

Lily mimicked the maneuver.

John climbed up into the driver's seat of the carriage as Hannah, Job and Queen Esther found their places in it.

The head guard approached the queen. "Your Majesty, can I persuade you to let a guard patrol escort you?"

"It will not be necessary. Everyone should prepare for the final day. I declare a fast and prayer! Do not eat until these times of trouble have passed." The queen turned to her companions. "Onward to Abar Mountain!"

From beneath the white tree, Elstar stood and walked toward Lily and then beside Victormane. Lily clenched the reins and gripped the horse's withers, passing the balsam tree where Pity-Petty had died. The group left the oval courtyard under fading yellow and gold streaks in the sky.

"Did I hear you have two siblings?" asked Joseph as he rode beside Lily.

"Yes. I have two brothers, an older and a younger one."

"A rose between two thorns," said Paul from behind, chuckling.

"I guess you could say so," said Lily, laughing. Two monarch butterflies landed on each of Victormane's ears. Lily swayed with the horse's gait.

"I have eleven brothers," said Joseph.

"Wow. That's a big family," said Lily.

The group passed rows of stores, a theater, several large buildings, and a church from which sweet singing could be heard. When the main road through the royal city of Jerul brought them to the back gate, Lily squinted at two men waiting on horses. Under a stone arch, one man seemed too large for the horse beneath him while the other was familiar.

Lily gawked. "Is that Finn?"

Deborah leaned forward on her horse. "I think it is. He keeps showing up, doesn't he?"

Lily glanced at Deborah wondering if she knew why Finn kept showing up, and then at Elstar trotting beside Victormane. He didn't look up but she remembered his nudge in the garden.

"Where are you all headed?" Finn asked when the group arrived at the gate.

John steadied the two-horse team. "Caper."

"My friend Buzz and I are headed there. Mind if we ride along?" Buzz's horse sidestepped under the weight of his heavy, cumbersome body.

"Not at all. Please do." John maneuvered the carriage through the gate

Job looked up at the gate as they passed through. "The Caper Gate. Look at this fine structure. I said to myself—what a well-built edifice. Finn, didn't your father work on it?"

Finn shrugged. "I heard he did."

Lily followed the caravan through the gate, Victormane steady and strong. She admired the craftsmanship of the gate then heard an eagle's cry. The bird soared on currents coming off Abar Mountain and between patches of gray clouds and streaks of lavender, the gold and yellow bands now gone.

"Your father was a good man," added John.

Buzz snorted. "Good man? I might have to go ahead and disagree with you on that." But when Finn scowled at Buzz, he stretched out his hand as if to stop traffic. "But that was a long time ago. Good ole Chucking Charlie. Yeah, he was a good man."

Buzz swatted Finn's arm. "That reminds me. Remember old Mrs. Clegg? She lived next to you—the one you robbed clean. Remember her? Rich as all get out! Filthy Cackling Clegg—that's what we used to call her. Well, she up and died. And get this: she left her house to my mother's sister. Can you believe that?"

Finn turned away, looking at an ugly shrub in the middle of a weedy field. Only the thud of hooves on the dirt road filled the moments that followed. Lily fidgeted with the reins. Was Finn sad that Mrs. Clegg died? Was he mad at himself for stealing?

Mary steered her horse around a hole in the road. "I'm sure you know that stealing is wrong. Wrong is wrong."

Buzz chuckled.

Wrong is wrong. Lily remembered writing a cruel poem about a girl in school. The beloved teacher caught Lily and she had to own up to her wrongdoing. The sad look in the teacher's eyes made Lily sorry for what she had done.

Lily wanted to give Finn hope even though everyone makes mistakes. Then words often uttered from Lily's mother bubbled to the surface of her mind and overflowed out her mouth. "Love covers a multitude of sins, though."

Elstar kicked his back feet up then pranced around in front of Victormane.

Buzz wiped his nose on his sleeve. "Pfft! What? Love doesn't cover anything."

Lily's nostrils flared. Buzz was as irritating as a scratchy sweater. No. More than that. But Lily couldn't think of what at the moment. She was too upset at Buzz.

"You're right, Lily," said John, his red sweater lessening the gray sky behind him. "Love does cover a multitude of sins.

It was love that moved our creator to send us Elstar. Those who have ears to hear, let them hear!"

John's words sunk deep into Lily's heart. *For God so loved the world, that He gave His only begotten Son, that whosoever believes in Him shall not perish but have everlasting life.*

"In fact," added John, "love is the only force capable of turning an enemy into a friend."

Lily half-smiled, feeling a small victory. She didn't have to listen to Buzz or agree with him.

Victormane grabbed a mouthful of tall grass beside the road, his strong neck jerking to the side to rip the grass, roots and all, and he chomped on the meal as he walked.

Hannah leaned over the edge of the carriage. "I'm thankful for the privilege of prayer. By it, joy has been realized. It has been my strength."

Remembering a song, Lily quoted the lyric. "The joy of the Lord is my strength."

Buzz spit, making Lily cringed, hoping a breeze didn't bring any residue her way.

"Buzz," snapped Finn, "do you think you can have some manners?"

"Oh, sor-ry." He put his hand over his heart and fluttered his eyelashes then sneered at Finn. "Your aunt doesn't believe in prayer and she goes to church."

Finn sneered back. "How do you know?"

"Cause she said so," said Buzz. "You want to hear what I say? You got to make your own way. Grab life by the horns and growl! Cause no one gives a huffing iota anyway." Buzz looked up at the sky. "Hey, isn't it supposed to be getting brighter as the day goes on?"

Lily looked at Hannah and both of them raised their eyebrows at each other.

Finn turned to Lily. "But *you* believe in prayer, don't you?"

Lily met Finn's eyes and nodded.

The country road came alongside a flowing river. Paul rode beside Lily. "Here is the Kerith River which means we're almost to the town of Caper, just ahead in that forest."

Lily peered ahead. "How long will it take to go through the Gosi Pass?"

"About an hour, depending on the snow."

Buzz perked up on his horse. "The Gosi Pass? What in tarnation are you going through there for? It only leads to Sapphira's Wasteland."

"We go to see the fulfillment of prophecy," said Joseph.

"Sapphira's Wasteland?" repeated Lily. The very words made her stomach churn. She took a long breath and exhaled.

Buzz shuddered. "Wouldn't catch me there! It's worse than Cush!"

Lily's throat constricted until she felt Deborah's soft touch on her arm and heard her words of comfort.

"There is a peace that passes understanding even in times of trouble. That's how we go to the end."

The rhythmic horse clopping and river rapid sounds soothed Lily as Elstar pranced between the horses. She thought of Psalm twenty-three and the part about going through the valley of the shadow of death but not fearing any

146

evil. Then she repeated Deborah's words: "Peace that passes understanding."

Buzz barked out, "End, sh-mend! There ain't no end. Don't get worked up over this bad weather. Like any gray day, the sun will shine again. It's just another day in paradise. Pfft! Peace that passes understanding? What kind of malarkey is that? There ain't no peace. The only understanding anyone needs is how much you can get in this world before you check out!"

More words from Buzz Lily knew she didn't have to agree with.

Buzz turned to Finn. "Hey, I went to see that sawed-off buddy of yours over in Ephra. He's going to find you 'cause he says you owe him big."

Finn looked away from Buzz, quiet and unchanged. Lily followed Finn's gaze to an empty field under a growing gray sky. *Why is he so quiet? What is he thinking?*

"I know you got that court hearing thing," continued Buzz, throwing up a dismissive hand wave, "but you'll ace that, hands down."

Deborah gave Buzz an inquisitive look. That look held power and reality, the traits of a judge. Lily remembered Deborah was a judge, and maybe even the one who would be handling Finn's case.

Buzz couldn't be more wrong. He was not the one to ask questions of because none of his answers would be any good. Why did he have to travel with them? Why couldn't he go somewhere else? But did Lily have these same questions for Finn, questions she used to have? She didn't think she did.

147

Under purple clouds billowing off the peak of Abar Mountain, Lily felt a chill. She had prayed for Finn's salvation. It was her goal to help him.

The clouds mixed with dark blue swirls over the town of Caper as the road turned from the Kerith River. Lily thought she would want to help Buzz too, if she could.

They entered into a stand of evergreen trees. Wood smoke permeated the dank air from log homes. They would need their coats soon and maybe a scarf or two.

In front of a barn with the image of a cross and coat hanger on top—the Gambrel, an old man with long ears chopped wood. When he saw the travelers, he leaned his ax against the barn door and wiped his hands on his bib overalls.

"Got a storm brewing." He pointed to the darkening sky and then at Briella. "I'm sure you are aware that you have butterflies all over you."

Briella gave a nod. "They are always with me."

The man frowned and a wrinkle appeared between his eyebrows. "I see. Well, where ya'll headed?" He wiped his forehead with a handkerchief.

"To the plateau," said Queen Esther from the carriage.

The man dropped his handkerchief. "Oh, not too many people venture there." He bent down to pick it up, stumbled, and then stared at the queen. "Your Majesty! Please excuse me. I did not know it was you." He promptly bowed.

Queen Esther smiled and scooped her hand. "Please stand."

Buzz leaned over the neck of his horse. "My good man, where's a good place to eat? I'm so hungry my stomach thinks

148

my throat's cut."

"That would be Paddy's Pub." The man pointed down the road. "On Main Street, past the mill. You can't miss it."

Buzz clicked his tongue and spurred his mount toward the town, leaving the group. But Finn stayed with the group.

The old logger tugged at his overalls. "You seem a strange lot for these parts, begging your pardon, Your Majesty. I'm sure the guards stationed at the plateau will enjoy having visitors, that's for sure. I'm sure they can tell you that. Hope you brought warm clothes. I hear tell there's snow still in the Gosi Pass."

"We did," said Mary.

"Why are you heading to the plateau, if I may be so bold?" asked the man, inspecting his fingernails.

John steadied the team of horses. "It's due to great news! The White Tree has bloomed. Elstar has appeared and travels with us as we speak."

The man ceased picking his fingernails. He looked at Briella once more, as if noticing her for the first time. "Briella the White? You are Briella the White? I should have known." He stepped back. "The butterflies. Of course. The eagles must have flown. And the lamb has appeared? Elstar? Well, I … I have some things to do. I … I wish you well! All of you! And praise Elstar!" The man turned and ran to his house as fast as he could.

"I think he must be glad," said John. He chuckled then steered the carriage toward the town. "Those who have ears to hear, let them hear!"

149

Lily rode with her friends in a caravan down Caper's main street lined with spruce trees while Elstar trotted beside them. The sky grew darker as their horses walked past the general mercantile facing the saw mill. They caught up with Buzz as he lollopped up the stairs to the door of Paddy's Pub.

Buzz patted his stomach and called to the group. "I smell me some sausage and eggs. Time to get some grub from the pub before this storm hits." He looked up at the dark sky then pushed through the doors of the establishment.

Finn tied up his horse and followed Buzz but stopped at the door and looked back with a peculiar look on his face. "Aren't you all coming?"

Paul shook his head. "No. We're fasting."

The smell of bacon wafting out the door made Lily bite her lip. Her grumbling stomach made her think about going into the most-likely dirty pub with Finn and Buzz, but she emptied that thought from her head. Besides, she wanted to please her friends.

"Suit yourself." Finn eyed Lily then turned and stepped into the pub.

Paul turned to the group. "There is a fresh spring up the road. We'll stop there to have a drink. In the end, there will be a feast like none other."

Deborah rubbed her arms. "But until then, I think it's time to get the coats on."

By a row of cedar trees beside Paddy's Pub, John parked the carriage and Queen Esther stepped onto the road. "My, the cold air settles on this town. Our ascension up the mountain road will only prove colder. Dress warmly, my friends."

"And the hours ahead will only grow darker," said John. "Let us conserve our oil, though, for when it is most needed." He and Joseph detached the tethered horses and the team from the parked carriage.

Philip opened the trunk lid and he and Lily passed out coats to everyone before donning their own.

Hannah finished buttoning her coat. "Let's walk our horses for a while. There is still enough light to see the road under this darkening sky and it would be good to get the blood flowing in our legs."

As the group started down the road, Philip and Lily found Hannah's bag of hats, mittens, scarves, and a copy of the Old Text before closing the lid of the trunk and joining the others.

"We'd better bring Hannah's bag," said Philip.

Philip fished through the bag and chose a hat. He pulled down an orange yarn cap with ear pockets and fit his ears into them. Lily giggled then picked a red wool hat with ear pockets that hung on either side. She swished her head back and forth so the pockets flung out when the extra material hit the sides of her head. She added the red scarf.

Philip closed the trunk lid and then put a finger to his lips to indicate quiet. On the other side of the cedar trees, a door at the back of the pub had just slammed shut.

"I'm telling you, Finn, it's worth millions! We'd be set for life. I know you're interested. Who'd miss out on a chance like this?"

Lily and Philip quietly snuck to the cedar trees and peered through the branches. Buzz and Finn were arguing on the back deck of the pub. Buzz bit off a piece of meat from a drumstick.

151

Finn circled round to face Buzz. "What about Briella? She's tougher than she looks."

"That Butterfly Bimbo? I'm not afraid of her! I can lift that necklace without anyone knowing. Now's our chance. There's no guards!" Buzz chewed his meat. After a few moments, he waved it in front of Finn's face. "You don't *like* them, do you?"

Finn glared at Buzz in silence.

Buzz stepped back, his mouth agape. "You *do*?"

"I'm not saying I do. But think. Why would they go up Abar Mountain all the way to Sapphira's Wasteland in this weather?"

"Cause they're nuts?" Buzz took another bite of the drumstick.

Finn scowled before giving Buzz a serious look. "Maybe. But I'm gonna find out. I've got nothing to lose."

Buzz's face turned red and he jabbed a crooked finger into Finn's chest. "Well, just so you know, I'm making this trip count. That necklace will be mine!"

Chapter Eleven

To Conquer the Mountain

Victormane's hooves dug into the road. Clods of dirt kicked up behind him as he carried Lily down the shadowy road. Her coat flapped behind her as she leaned into the stallion's powerful neck jerking her forward and backward. She and Philip raced between thick woodlands on either side of the road.

"I can't believe they want to steal Queen Esther's necklace!" Lily yelled between Victormane's strides.

"Yes, but Finn might be changing!" Philip yelled back.

153

Down the road, the group waited for them, each holding the reins of their horse. Arriving, Lily pulled back on the reins as Victormane let out a sneeze.

"Is everything all right?" asked Hannah.

"No!" panicked Lily. "Finn and Buzz ..." she looked at Queen Esther, "...they want to steal your necklace!"

Queen Esther touched her necklace with her fingertips. She paused before speaking with a slight grin on her face. "If

154

they succeed, they succeed. We are heading to a grander time, which I wish they would be a part of, but that is up to them." From a rock, she mounted her horse, sitting sideways, and her long fur coat draped over her legs. "Stay the course, even in these dire times. Self-control, to the very end, I say."

John took a breath and let it out before mounting his horse. "Such is the heart which has the potential to do incredible good or terrible things. We can't give up hope on Finn or Buzz. They might yet come to their senses."

Deborah nodded and stroked the neck of her horse. "Maintain peace amidst folly."

Peace amidst folly. Okay. It is better than revenge, and doesn't the Bible say 'blessed are the peacemakers'?. Lily breathed easier in the safety of the group and especially when Elstar nodded his head and pranced around. She wished everyone could see his glowing fleece and springy dance steps.

The raging flow of Kerith River ushered them out of the cold town of Caper. Beneath a dark purple sky, Briella, Job, and Deborah rode their horses at the front of the processional. John and Queen Esther followed, their horse's tails swishing behind them as they talked. Joseph and Philip steered around holes in the dirt road while Elstar trotted between them. And Lily, Mary, Hannah, and Paul spanned the width of the road at the back of the caravan. Soon, they came to a large waterfall surrounded by evergreens engulfed heavy in mist.

Elstar hopped onto a rock and his hooves clicked as he made his way to the top where he lay down. He watched everyone from a high viewpoint.

Briella dismounted beside a pool of water. "Here is Kerith Falls. Let us get a drink and water our horses." She led her horse to the water's edge and dropped the reins then knelt beside a spring, cupped her hands, and drank a few draughts. "Oh, that is very good!"

Lily led Victormane to the pool beside a rock near citrusy-smelling tree branches. Her dry mouth longed for cool relief. She stepped to the spring but turned back when she heard galloping horses coming down the road.

"Here they are!" Buzz called out, leaning back. "The gang! Sorry back there. Had to get some breakfast. It was good enough food, although the sweet rolls weren't too good. A bit stale if you ask me. Still, wolfed it down like it was my last meal!"

Lily glanced at Mary with a wrinkle in her forehead. *Who's he talking to?* Mary raised her eyebrows and gave half a smile but it washed away when her sad eyes looked down.

Why is Mary sad? He's up to no good. As a matter of fact, he's planning to steal the necklace. Who knows what else he's planning.

Buzz jumped off his horse and budged ahead of Lily to the spring. "Not the best place in town—that Paddy's Pub. I'll have to try that other place. What was it called? Oh yeah, Cheese Joey's."

Finn got off his horse. "Pipe down! No one wants to hear what you ate. Excuse us. We lack in … " Finn searched for the right word, " … grace. I wanted to ask why you all are heading up Abar Mountain."

"It's because of the white tree prophecy," said John. "When the tree blooms, Elstar will be fully known on the same

156

day at three o'clock. Since the tree bloomed this very morning, we travel to see the prophecy's fulfillment."

Finn's mouth dropped open. "So, you're going to the Gambrel?"

"You know of the prophecy?"

"I've heard of it."

Buzz ducked under a tree branch hanging over the spring and spit into the water just above Lily. "He never put much stock in it, though."

Lily studied the flow of the water, seeing where the spit might be. She waited until she was sure good water had flushed out any residue and then she and Mary cupped their hands and drank clear water while Elstar continued to watch from the rock.

"I'm curious about it, though," said Finn.

"You're welcome to come with us," said John.

"And me?" bellowed Buzz. "Can I tag along?"

John gave Buzz a stern look. Was he going to tell him his plan was known by everyone? Was he going to tell him he would be arrested? But he gave a small smile and said, "Yes."

Lily took one last handful of water before retrieving Victormane. When she turned him around, Buzz planted his horse in front of her, pinning her and Victormane against a rock and blocking her way. It was tempting to yell 'Get out of the way!' but she kept her mouth shut. She thought how cool it would be if Victormane plowed Buzz down but that wouldn't be very Christian. So, she waited for Buzz, staring at the dirt path.

157

Finn stopped talking with John and yipped at Buzz, "Move, Buzz! You're blocking the way."

Buzz spun around to Lily. "Oh, sor-ry. Am I in your way?" He moved to one side, pretending to care.

Lily avoided eye contact as she passed Buzz who swung his hand out gracefully for her to proceed.

"This way, princess," said Buzz.

Lily climbed up on Victormane's back with Philip's help before catching a nasty look from Buzz. She looked away and stared at the rough bark of a tree. *I can't stand him.*

Briella mounted her horse. "Let us begin the long ascent up Abar Mountain. There is still enough light lingering in the sky, but the time will come when the way will be too dark."

Buzz kept eyeing Queen Esther. *I'm sure he knows he can't outrun Philip on a horse. If Buzz and Finn do anything, they won't get far, although Finn doesn't seem to be interested in the necklace. But if so, they will be caught and maybe turned into a statue. Or set on fire.*

Elstar bleated and hopped off the rock. He circled around Briella's horse while Queen Esther wrapped her indigo shawl tighter around her neck. Then Elstar glanced at Lily. His prancing gait encouraged her to continue.

Job stroked his beard. "Until that time, we will conserve our fuel and be patient, or as some say 'loonngg…suffering'." He tapped his horse's sides to move forward.

Buzz snorted. "Long-suffering? I ain't suffering for nothing, short or long!"

Lily grimaced. *This trip is not going to be easy.*

The group started up the rutted road. Lily steered Victormane into the processional while Elstar walked along.

They rode their horses over a carpet of pine needles beside a grove of tall pines.

"Hey, I got a joke," said Buzz, holding up his index finger. "Who doesn't need a good laugh, right? There was this priest who went up into the Realm. EL opened the gate and let him in and he made him a tuna fish sandwich, which they ate. Then, the priest looked down through the floor grate to the Abyss and saw all the people there eating steak, prime rib, and lobster. The priest asked, 'How come we're only eating tuna fish sandwiches?' EL replied, 'When there's only two of us, why cook?'"

Finn grinned.

Buzz guffawed at Finn. "You thought that was pretty funny, didn't you?"

The grin on Finn's face disappeared. "I don't know if that's the best joke to be telling, though."

Buzz raised his eyebrows at Finn. "But you did think it funny."

Finn looked away.

Mary frowned. "Well, I didn't think it was funny."

Buzz squared his shoulders and tightened the reins around his hand. "Well, I'd rather laugh with my friends in the Abyss than cry in the Realm. I'm gonna be wherever my friends are, deary." He smacked the horse's side with the excess of rein and moved forward to ride with Queen Esther.

Lily grew dismayed when she met Mary's sad eyes again. "I didn't like it either."

"Now, now," said Job, "don't let that stupid joke bother either of you. There might still be a change. Some people are just tougher than a pine knot. We travel on and keep waiting for the moment of renewal."

Mary adjusted her scarf, which she had retrieved from Hannah's bag earlier as they rode. She pulled it tighter to ward off the chill coming down the mountain while Lily pulled her hat down, the ear pockets no longer entertaining.

Job's words made Lily remember a Bible verse her mother had on the refrigerator back home and wishing to say something positive, she shared it. "'Those who wait upon the Lord shall renew their strength. They shall mount up with wings like eagles.'"

"You speak well," said Mary as the group passed through dark woods.

Lily swayed with the horse's gait. "Thank you."

Elstar jumped over a branch in the road, his white fleece glowing bright.

Finn came up alongside Lily. "Buzz is a knucklehead. Don't let him bother you."

Did Finn care about her now? Or was his concern a decoy? Was he just using her? Her heart told her, as her friends encouraged, to put up with long-suffering and aim for kindness and goodness. Lily half-smiled. "I won't."

The thuds of horse hooves echoed off tree trunks as Victormane flicked his ears. Then Lily asked Finn, "Is Buzz his *real* name?"

Finn chuckled. "No. When he was little, he pretended to be a bee running around stinging everyone at the Bundlemann family reunion. I guess the name 'Buzz' stuck."

"Buzz Bundlemann?" Lily suppressed a grin.

160

"The one and only." Finn leaned from his horse and spoke quieter. "His real name is Marion but don't tell him I told you. He'd skin me alive."

Lily smiled. "Marion?"

"Sh. Keep that to yourself."

"Okay. Have you guys been friends for a long time?"

"We grew up together." Finn looked into the woods. "After my mother passed away, he went his way and I went mine." He looked back at Lily. "She died from leprosy, a skin disease."

"I'm sorry."

Finn shrugged.

"And your father?"

"He drank himself into oblivion. He couldn't deal with her death. But then someone told me he cleaned up and stopped drinking. A few years ago, though, he was found dead under a tree, dragged by a horse. They're both gone now. Not much I can do about that."

Buzz turned and called back, "You still got me!"

"Pfft! You're only a friend when you want something," Finn called back to him.

Buzz turned his horse and trotted back. "What is this? Pick-on-Buzz day?" His horse neighed and tossed his head in the air. "Look at that! Even my horse hates me! Did I hear the Bundlemann family name back here?" Buzz glanced at Lily. "Did he tell you how I was this bumblebee brat-of-a-boy buzzing around my bigger brothers being the life of the Bundlemann family barbeque? It was all fun and games 'til I ran into the dessert table and sent Aunt Beulah's strawberry pie flying smack into my father's face."

Finn laughed. "I bet Bundlemann was boiling!"

Buzz swatted Finn's arm. "Darn tootin he was! I never seen anyone with a redder face. You don't want to mess with him, especially when he's drunk. Man, I haven't seen the old folks in years but I can't says I miss them."

Joseph rode along. "Why not give them a visit."

"Nah," said Buzz. "I met this doctor guy who told me to leave home. So I did."

"Doctor? asked Finn.

"Yeah. He's real good."

"Hold on there, Buzz," said Finn. "How long did you know this doctor?"

Buzz tilted his head. "About thirty minutes. Point is: everything he said was right." He shot an angry look at Joseph. "Why am I talking this nonsense with the likes of you?"

Cold air brushed against Lily's face and she shifted on Victomane's back.

Finn gave Buzz an angry look. "We're just making conversation here. Besides, maybe your parents weren't great but there's way worse."

Buzz snarled at Finn. "Yeah, well you didn't have to live with them. I wash my hands of them just like the doc said." Buzz spit.

Finn glared at Buzz, causing him to hold up a hand like a traffic cop. "I'm sorry." Buzz looked at Lily. "But you see, little lady, you got to toughen up or the world will spit you out. I'm trying to give you character, put some meat on your bones."

Lily's nostrils flared. *Meat on my bones?* She didn't want to get into an argument with Buzz Marion Bundlemann. Lily knew she didn't need the kind of meat he thought she needed. As she rode with Joseph, she remembered the word 'kindness' again written beneath Joseph's mentor in the dining room of his stately home. She scrambled, searching for something to say, something positive. Maybe even something kind. "Character is good," she said, "and having the right kind is best."

Buzz snarled. "You can't let your parents rule over you forever. At some point, you got to break away on your own trail." He rode ahead again, mumbling something.

Lily stewed. Her chest constricted. She no longer felt cold on her face because her cheeks were warm.

"There is some truth to that," said Finn. "You'll have to leave your parents some day."

Joseph edged closer to Lily. "But that doesn't mean you have to be rude to your parents. It is honorable to honor your parents."

Lily's lungs eased as tightness subsided. She was glad to have Joseph as her friend. She faced him, smiled, and nodded.

Elstar skirted around them again.

Finn paused. "Well, that's true too. I doubt Buzz has seen his parents in a long time. They were good to him."

"Maybe you could visit them sometime," suggested Lily. "Let them know how Buzz is doing. I'm sure they'd love to see you and hear about their son."

Finn chuckled. "I'd have to do some serious sugarcoating!" Then he bit his lip. "But if that prophecy you all speak of comes true today, I don't have time."

Chapter Twelve

Under Dark Skies

The group ascended the narrow mountain road between thin, scraggly trees on both sides as they proceeded in a single line. The woods lacked luster in the gray and darker gray surroundings, making them look like an x-ray image to Lily. But she kept her eyes on Elstar's glowing fleece even though she was the only one who could see him. She wished her friends could see the light he produced from his own body. His dainty, sure steps led the way.

John called back. "We're coming to a pull-off area. Let's light the lanterns there."

"Agreed," said Job. "The wind is picking up. Best to get them lit."

Lily and the group gathered in the pull-off area beside a shabby row of thin fir trees which did little to block the cold mountain air. Job touched his right knee when his foot reached the ground. "Oh, this knee! My body is a barometer."

"Oh dear," said Hannah. "We're not spring chickens anymore. Just take it slow." She climbed down from her horse. "We must bear this last stretch of the way as best we can."

"Yes, we must," said John. "The crowning day is near. Our current time is almost over."

Lily parked Victormane beside Mary's horse, brought her legs together, and then jumped down. Wind blew across her face and the ear pockets of her hat fluttered. She placed the side of her face close to Victormane's neck for warmth and shelter.

Job reached into his pocket and pulled out a flint stone and a knife then un-wrapped a leather pouch and held up a small stick with cloth on the end. When Job lit it, light reflected on his face. Job and Joseph began lighting the lanterns that hung from the horses' chest harnesses. The glow of the light reflected on the ground.

Buzz jumped down from his horse and rubbed his hands together to get them warm. "How much further to this accursed Caper Post?" He blew air into his cupped hands.

Hannah passed her bag. "Here, Buzz. I have extra hats and mittens. You're welcome to them."

"Thank you, ma'am." Buzz ruffled through the bag and pulled out a hat, scarf, and mittens which he donned.

"Finn, help yourself, said Hannah, motioning for Buzz to pass the bag to him.

"Thank you." Finn wrapped a scarf around his neck and tucked the ends into the lapels of his coat. Then he flipped up the collar of his jacket.

Apparently not bothered by the cold wind, Hannah said, "Can you believe we're going to feast with Elstar himself today?"

John held the lantern hanging in front of Victormane as

Joseph lit it. "That's our creator's promise. What do we have without hope of a promise fulfilled?"

"Nothing," answered Joseph. "But because of Elstar's kindness, we can dine in the Realm today."

Buzz swung out his arms, hitting Lily in the arm. "Everyone will go to the Realm, then, because the creator wouldn't let anyone go to the Abyss, being so patient and kind. You said it yourself."

While a cold gust swirled around Lily's head and beat against her pants, she knew Buzz hit her on purpose. *Can't he see I'm standing here? I know he can see me.*

Buzz eyed Lily from her hat to her boots.

Lily stared back. She calculated the mass of his shoulders and chest. He could clobber her if he wanted to.

Buzz pinned Lily with a glare. "Do you have something to say, princess?"

She wanted to say: *Buzz, you're a jerk*, especially for just now hitting her. Instead, she moved away from him and closer to Briella, organizing her thoughts and trying to maintain self-control. "I … I don't think that's quite right, Buzz. I mean, in my world …"

Buzz followed Lily.

Lily met Buzz's steady pupils and traced the creases in his face to his long ears as her mind worked to explain. "…in my world, it's not like that."

Buzz squinted. "Well, maybe your creator isn't patient and kind." His biting words matched the biting wind.

"No. He definitely is," she shot back then saw Elstar lying down beneath trees at the back of the turn-off.

168

"How do you know, princess?"

Lily hated the name but she focused, repeating Buzz's question in her head. *How do I know? How do I know what? That Elstar is patient and kind? That Jesus is patient and kind?* As she stared at Buzz, Lily thought the others could answer him.

John put in. "Spoken or written, a creator's power cannot be altered. When he says something will happen, it will happen. His word is so powerful that he cannot lie."

Yes. Like what happened to Adam and Eve. They were told not to eat from a certain tree in the Garden of Eden or else they would die. But they disobeyed and ate. So they had to die. An all-powerful God has an all-powerful word.

Queen Esther's horse rested its head on her shoulder. "I think it as authority. The king's words can mean life or death. His command will be carried out."

"So," continued Buzz, "this so-called creator will kill off what he made? What a guy!"

The biting wind blowing across Lily's body made her shiver. She eyed Buzz again, seeing that he waited for her to say something. She formed her thoughts again.

"My creator almost destroyed everyone in my world. There was a flood. God covered the whole earth with water. But He chose not to end creation permanently. He told this man named Noah to build an ark and take his family inside plus two of every kind of animal. They got in and floated on the water until God let the waters go back down." Lily paused. "Years later, God sent His Son, Jesus. If people believe in Jesus, they will be saved like Noah."

"Saved?" Buzz's ears darted back. "From what?"

Lily scuffed her boot on the ground before looking up at him. "From wrath."

Paul mounted his horse. "When all evil will be destroyed."

Hannah raised her scarf to block the wind. "The wrath is not a good thing to face without a mediator."

Paul gathered the reins of his horse. "No one will survive the wrath unless they are saved." His words soared on a gust of wind.

"I wish everyone would believe in Elstar," said Mary, "so they wouldn't have to face the wrath."

Buzz threw down his arms. "Pfft! Hogwash!"

John looked sadly at the ground before mounting his horse. "We'd better get going. There's a dusting of snow already on the road."

Buzz bumped Lily again and said in a low voice, "What do you think you can do with your stupid story? I think *you* should go back home."

Lily clenched her jaw. After watching him mount his horse, she stared at the ground. *Maybe I should go home. Why keep going? I'm a target that arrows are being shot at!* She glanced at Briella. She could send her home right now. Lily looked back at the ground, tired of dealing with Finn and Buzz's persecution.

But Mary spoke gently to Buzz. "You really should listen. There is a time coming real soon …"

"I'll take my chances, deary." Buzz interrupted her.

Lily frowned after him as he kicked his horse to proceed, and then she looked at Mary, who let out a heavy sigh. Mary kept her arms and legs close to her body to keep warm. "Come on, Lily. Let's go."

Elstar rubbed Lily's leg and she knelt to caress him, his warmth passing through her body. She whispered to him, "I'm not sure I want to keep going but you've brought me this far. I shouldn't give up because Buzz and Finn are rude, although Finn seems less rude. Actually, he hasn't been too rude at all. I've got to forgive them like Jesus would want me to."

She sighed, her mind clear with determination, then stood to catch Finn watching her. He looked like he was about to say something but instead gestured nicely with his arm for her to go before him.

As the horse caravan left the pull-off area and light from their lanterns spread out before their horses on the lightly-dusted snowy road, Lily pushed traces of doubt out of her mind. Her trust in God's Word grew deeper roots as they passed shrubby trees in the wind gusts of the higher elevation. The wind howling over scraggly trees didn't throw Lily off course.

Buzz called out from behind. "Right about now, I wish I were fishing at Warbler Swamp on a warm, sunny day instead of riding up this frozen path in this freezing wind. Yup, warm Warbler Swamp. Finn, were you there last week? I could have sworn I saw you."

"No, I wasn't there."

"You should have been there, man. Bass were biting. So were the pickerel. But since you never catch anything, probably would have been a wasted day. You still got that old rod?"

Finn nodded.

Buzz continued. "I hate to tell you but you need to upgrade, man. I've been there twice and you can pretty much

171

fish Warbler Swamp. Did you hear about Snake? What an epic story he had! He caught five record bass. Won the tournament, and that's in spite of what he ended up doing. I told him not to eat those oysters 'cause his intestines would coagulate but, he did anyways. Heaved during his last cast. Won the championship anyways, though. Next day, he was sicker than a dog but he healed up pretty good. I was impressed. You know, some guys call him a 'puffer' 'cause he brags about himself all the time. He says he's gonna get into trapping. Said his cousin told him he would make the best trapper because of all his tracking knowledge with deer. But I don't think he'd be very good at it, not if you ask me."

Lily pulled her hat down and re-tucked her scarf, letting out a moan from Buzz's mumbling mish-mash of monologue. Wind ripped through her without the protection of tall evergreen trees. But thankfully, the gale also sent most of Buzz's foolish words flying off the mountain. Elstar marched ahead, his footprints in the snow seen only by Lily in the light of the lantern hanging from Victormane's chest harness.

Paul pointed down the valley. "There is Jerul—what you can see of it."

Lily turned her head stiffly so her scarf wouldn't fall and let the freezing air sting her bare neck.

"The view is usually incredible on a clear day but not today," said Paul.

Mary pointed to the sky. "Look at those!"

Lily sunk her head into her shoulders as dark clouds poured over the mountain like huge snakes seeking their prey. Her stomach churned and she forced a swallow.

172

"It won't take long before Jerul is covered in darkness," said Paul.

Lily quivered. But then she reminded herself that Elstar had easily destroyed Sayta the Formidable.

There were no more trees in the higher heights of Abar Mountain, not even straggly, stunted ones. As they passed vertical rows of icicles that clung to the mountain wall, Lily knew none of her friends traveled with dismay in their hearts. The wind kicked up snow on the mountain and tossed it around her head. She shielded her eyes in the blowing snow, peering ahead at lights from two windows shining across the road.

"There's the Caper Post!" called John.

"Yes!" Lily cheered beneath her scarf with frozen bits of breath condensation. She didn't know how much more cold she could stand.

On a ledge of Abar Mountain, Lily could see a building and a barn nestled into the rock. A large pile of wood in pyramid formation filled a space near a cliff. Two guards marched out holding torches blazing in the dark air, the first wearing a heavy fur coat with an ammunition belt across his chest and the other with a coat and fur-covered boots.

"What is your business?" demanded the first guard while the other rested his hand on the handle of a knife at his waist.

Briella's voice carried on the wind. "I am Briella the White. We wish to pass through the Gosi Pass to the plateau."

The guard lifted his torch. "Briella the White—the one who waits for the appearance of the lamb on Lambstone Mountain?"

"Elstar has appeared and travels with us. The White Tree bloomed this morning!" In the wind, Briella's butterflies clung to individual strands of her white hair.

The guard staggered backwards with a perplexed look that changed to delight. A smile spread across his face and he placed his hand over his heart. He turned to the other guard, his torch swinging out pieces of fire that fell on the snow. "That would explain why the Wasteland is darker than usual."

Joseph stepped down from his horse. "Are you Habakkuk?"

"I am. And this is Private Wolff. You are welcome here if you honor Elstar."

"We do," said John. "With all our heart."

"Good. Private Wolff will assist you with your horses." Habakkuk gestured with his head as Private Wolff walked toward the barn. "This way."

After blowing out her lantern to conserve fuel, Lily patted Victormane and then followed the others out of the barn to the front door of the Caper Post, Elstar trotting beside her.

Habakkuk bowed to Queen Esther. "Please come in, Your Majesty. Please accept our humble accommodation."

Queen Esther smiled. "It is most accepted, Habakkuk."

The queen was followed by Finn. Then Elstar trotted behind him and before Lily. *How cute! He goes right in the building! I don't think anyone will mind.* She stopped, letting Elstar enter but then Buzz bumped into her from the right.

Buzz stepped back and bowed. "After you, Princess."

Lily snarled her lip and tamped down an angry response she'd like to make, letting the name-calling slide off her

174

shoulders. She told herself she would not let Buzz's rudeness or mockery get under her skin.

In the warm room, the strong smell of coffee filled Lily's nostrils. She unwound her scarf and hung it and her coat on a wooden peg beside Job's coat. Buzz bumped her again when he removed his coat.

Briella stepped between them. "Have a seat on the sofa, Lily."

With a don't-mess-with-me-because-an-angel-watches-over-me smile, Lily turned her back on Buzz and made her way to the sofa.

The coffee smell reminded Lily of the time her family visited the Johnsson's at Christmas time. She didn't like coffee. Now, cold and hungry, she would drink some, and maybe it would warm her up and give her fuel, especially if she added a lot of sugar. Deborah and Philip joined her on the sofa while Job rubbed his hands over a large cook stove.

I wonder how Job is handling this strong coffee smell, being a coffee lover.

Elstar lay down on a braided rug in front of the fire while Paul and Finn sat on the floor near him but they couldn't see him.

"Please, sit in the chairs." Habakkuk said to Paul and Finn pointing to empty overstuffed chairs.

Paul shook his head then raised his hand. "I'm fine."

Finn waved his hand, also not moving.

"Suit yourself," said Habakkuk.

Butterflies swarmed around the room, except for the ones on Briella's head. Buzz offered a chair to Queen Esther, which

175

was odd. He helped her with her scarf.

Private Wolff stood beside a cabinet of guns by the door. "We have coffee and bread and you're welcome to it."

Job looked up. "Thank you. It smells great! But we are praying and fasting until the end."

"What?" said Buzz. "Is that why you all didn't eat at Paddy's Pub? Well, I'm not fasting! Let me have some of that there cup of joe. Cold out there on this awful mountain."

Private Wolff poured coffee into a mug and handed it to Buzz.

Lily ignored her stomach rumbling. She wanted to fast like her friends. Then Lily met the queen's eyes as she touched her neck and put a finger to her lips, shaking her crowned head slightly. The necklace! It was gone! Briella, sitting next to the queen, also indicated quiet. *They don't want me to say anything?*

"Did you say this seat's available?" Buzz plopped himself in the overstuffed chair and tilted his head toward the food on the table. "I'll take some of that there bread too, if you don't mind."

Private Wolff handed him a slice while Habakkuk sat in the other chair watching Buzz closely before facing Briella. "So you say the white tree has bloomed. I knew this day would come! And you say Elstar travels with you?"

Briella's butterflies returned to her sleeves and flapped their wings. "Indeed." She gestured to Lily. "This is Lily. She can see Elstar."

Habakkuk leaned forward. "The Seer? Hmm. Do you see him now?"

Lily gave a nod.

176

"Where?"

Lily hesitated, wondering if the news would be upsetting to Habakkuk. She slowly pointed to Elstar resting on the floor in front of him.

The room grew quiet as Habakkuk studied the area. He folded his hands on his lap. When he looked back at Lily, she wished someone would say something.

John finally broke the silence. "The time has come. Redemption is near for the remnant of believers who will be redeemed. Those who have ears to hear, let them hear!"

"I am ready," said Habakkuk. "My life has been a long haul." He glanced at the rug. "Elstar knows what I speak of for he who made the heart knows the heart. Can we not do something? Can we not honor him right now?"

"Deborah has a sweet voice," said Briella.

"Then, sing! Sing for Elstar!" said Habakkuk.

Deborah cleared her throat. She sat up and let her soprano voice fill the room. Habakkuk closed his eyes as he listened. Then Job added his rich baritone voice to the song. Soon, Philip and Hannah blended their voices and Habakkuk leaned his head back against the overstuffed chair and sang—not as strong as the others, but still in tune.

Buzz ate his bread and slurped his coffee.

How can they keep on tolerating him?

After the last tone, Deborah faced Lily. "Would you sing with me?"

Shocked, Lily opened her eyes wide. She still wasn't comfortable singing in front of others.

"Yes, you," said Deborah. "Let's sing the song from the

177

jail." Deborah started the verse before Lily could protest from being singled-out. On the next phrase, Deborah tilted her head to coax Lily to sing. Lily matched the pitches Deborah sang and on the next phrase, added a harmony part. The two soprano voices blended together.

Elstar baaed and nodded his head when they finished their duet.

Habakkuk clapped his hands. "Excellent! We sing of his goodness!"

Lily knew of God's goodness. He had watched over her her whole life. Another Bible verse came to her mind and she shared it. "O sing unto the LORD a new song; for he hath done marvelous things."

Mary beamed at Lily, the flicker of the fire reflecting on her face. "Fine words."

The warmth of the fire spread all the way to Lily's toes. As they warmed up, Paul talked with Finn while Lily told Mary and Philip about the chorus in her school. Deborah and Joseph read the bindings of books on a shelf while Queen Esther, John, Job, and Hannah prayed in a back corner by bunk beds. Buzz ate the rest of the bread and perused the canned goods by the stove.

"Now that we are warmed up, let us proceed and enter the Gosi Pass," announced Briella.

Habakkuk put on his heavy coat and boots. "I will go with you through the pass to Sapphira's Wasteland. The wind has packed in layers of snow, two feet in some places. I know the way and I will guide you." He glanced where he thought Elstar was. "There is no need to fear as one stronger than us goes

178

before us."

Private Wolff asked Habakkuk, "Captain, is there any reason to guard the post anymore?"

Habakkuk pulled down a fur-lined hat.. "For the first time, no. And I'm not even taking my gun or ammunition belt."

"And the beacon? Should I light it?" asked Private Wolff.

Habakkuk nodded. "Light it. Let those who see it be prepared with the time that is left to them."

Buzz raised both his hands as if he were a referee halting a football game. "Ah, well, this is where I part ways, folks."

John stopped buttoning his coat. "Are you sure?"

"Positive," replied Buzz, standing up. "I couldn't be more positive—" he pointed to the fireplace, "– than wood burns."

The room became quiet while Buzz held his stand.

John waited. Was there sorrow in his face? He breathed slowly. Then Elstar moved, seen only by Lily. The lamb took on the same expression as John, and he and John waited on Buzz. When Buzz gave no change in his stance, John gave a nod. "So be it." John turned, opened the door, and left, Elstar and the group of friends following.

Lily put her coat, scarf, and mittens on. She headed for the door too but looked back at Buzz grasping Finn by the collar.

"Look," whispered Buzz, pulling out the necklace. He dangled the queen's blue diamond necklace in front of Finn's eyes. "I'm telling you, you could pay off all your debts." Buzz leaned into Finn. "Come on!"

Lily's heart pounded in her chest. *No, Finn. Don't do it.*

Finn's ashen face, like that of a ghost, seized Lily. Her heart rate increased. Was that pain that filled his eyes as he

179

stood in the strangled hold of his friend?

Lily shook her head to him. She knew she couldn't make Finn or Buzz do the right thing but she thought she'd try.

Finn looked back at Buzz and slowly pushed the necklace away with his hands.

Lily could hardly believe it. She grinned.

Buzz scrunched his brow and shot a nasty look at Lily. He looked back at Finn. "You've always been a lunkhead! Go with them!" he hissed as he pointed to the door. "When this weather clears, I'm gonna sell this necklace and be rich and you won't see *any* of it. I can promise you that!"

Lily's face could not have been brighter when she and Finn left the Caper Post together.

Victory won, Lily stood with Finn and their friends in front of the Gosi Pass holding their horses' reins. They watched raging flames shoot into the dark sky from the large wood-stacked beacon lit by Private Wolff. At the entrance to the Gosi Pass, Elstar waited between two walls of rock barely wide enough for a horse and its rider.

Chapter Thirteen

Till I Reach the End

"We're going in there?" Anguish twisted the features on Finn's face as he stared at the dark, empty entrance to the Gosi Pass.

Elstar's body lit the way. He entered, Habakkuk following, but no one could see Elstar except Lily. Light from Habakkuk's torch reflected on the iced walls of the narrow passageway.

Finn drew a deep breath and let it out. "I never dreamed I'd be going to Sapphira's Wasteland." Then he glanced back at the Caper Post.

Lily turned. Buzz was swinging the necklace in the window with a sinister smile on his face. Tightness gripped her chest. She searched for the right words. "Elstar is going *that* way," she pointed. "We've got to keep following *him*." Her words fumbled out. "You know, it's … it's just a necklace. You can't take it with you when you *die*." She studied his face, not sure if she should have emphasized the word 'die'. She added more brightly, "When I die, I'm going to Heaven. It's supposed to be really beautiful there."

Finn rubbed the reins in his hands. "Heaven, huh? That sounds like the Realm. Well, how did you know about the necklace, anyways?"

"Philip and I overheard you and Buzz on the deck at Paddy's Pub."

Finn glanced at Queen Esther entering the pass. He pointed and Lily turned to see the queen. "Did you tell her?"

"Yeah. Everyone knew you guys were trying to steal the necklace."

Finn turned pale.

Blood rushed through Lily's ears. "You won't be able to get Buzz to help you. He seemed sure you weren't getting any of that money. He'll cut you off." She paused, re-gaining her focus, using softer words. "Come with us. You've come this far. What's a little bit more? Maybe there's a kajillion blue diamond necklaces on the other side of that pass."

Finn half-laughed. "Buzz has been my friend for a long time, but, he *is* an idiot. I know how it will end with him: same old, same old. But something keeps tugging at me to go with

182

you. You and your friends." Finn smiled warmly. "Your resolve hasn't deterred."

Resolve? Is that the same thing as determination? Lily was glad Finn thought she had resolve and maybe she could show more. She found herself touching Finn's arm. Soft, reasonable words came out of her mouth. "Let's follow Elstar together and see where he leads."

Firelight from the beacon reflected in Finn's eyes. "Death. I never did really like that."

Lily grew serious. She thought of a quick reply. "That's why you got to know someone who has the words of life. For me, those are the words of Jesus. In your world, maybe it's from the words of your savior."

"We need to get going," said Paul, "if we're going to catch up with the others." He cupped his hands to boost Lily onto the back of Victormane.

As she mounted the horse, Lily saw Buzz peering out the window. Part of her wanted to stick her tongue out at him but she remembered reading in the Bible that Christians shouldn't do that. As he slowly backed away from the window and out of sight, leaving an empty space, the other part of Lily fretted over what might happen to Buzz.

Lily entered the narrow Gosi Pass behind Paul with Finn and Briella following. She crossed her arms and hunched her shoulders to trap her body heat as Victormane trudged through snow whipping up and circling around them. The light from their lanterns shot up walls of gray rock and reflected on the snow under a dark, shadowy sky. Lily tucked her head into her scarf. In the cold wind of Abar Mountain, they floundered behind Habakkuk who knew every twist and turn of the precarious way. After a while, the path grew wider and a large rock occupied the center of an opening big enough for the horses to gather around.

"This is Circle Rock, the halfway point," Habakkuk called out.

Like the circle of oak trees on Lambstone Mountain, the wind didn't blow in Circle Rock either. Elstar climbed to the top of the rock and overlooked the group in the light of their lanterns. Bluey fluttered above Briella's head like a sparkling blue light while the rest of the butterflies gathered in the air with him. He led them in a line around the rock from the base to the top. Bluey landed on Elstar's forehead while the six white butterflies lined up on the back of his head and the colorful ones along his back.

Mary leaned forward on her horse. "What is that?"

Hannah studied the butterflies. "Are they sitting on a branch?"

"But is there a branch?" asked Paul.

John shook his head. "No. There's no tree or bush."

Goosebumps formed on Lily's arms. *Now do they see Elstar?*

Mary grinned. "Look! They're moving."

Elstar made his way down Circle Rock and stopped in front of Finn.

Lily beamed. "It's Elstar. He's right in front of you, Finn."

Finn looked to the left and right of the 'branch'. He took off his mitten and extended his hand but he and everyone else couldn't see Elstar, only butterflies suspended in the air.

Paul grinned from ear to ear as they sprang up. "Short version of a long story, we live by faith! Faith is believing."

Lily nodded, remembering a Bible verse. "'The just shall live by faith'."

Finn put his mitten back on and looked at Lily.

Lily pulled her horse next to Finn's and added, "Faith is believing in your creator's word."

Finn tilted his head. "You have … a sense of …assurance. I mean, you seem so sure of what you believe."

"I am," said Lily.

Finn's eyebrows drew together. "But how can you *know?*"

Elstar laid down on Circle Rock while Lily formed her answer.

"I choose to believe. My faith is that I know Jesus loves me because He died on the Cross for my sins. He's the only one capable of saving, which makes Him the Savior. He died for me. You know, He's Creator God, in the flesh. Then, Jesus was raised from the dead on the third day. God is very powerful, even over death. He raised His Son from the dead."

Finn studied Lily, then said, "In the palace garden, you said someone was *in* you."

"The Holy Spirit. When I asked Jesus into my heart, He came in then too." The corners of Lily's mouth lifted as much as her eyebrows did.

Philip opened the Old Text and read a passage about Elstar. In the cold, still air, he explained how much Elstar loved his creation by dying on the Gambrel.

Like my faith. Jesus had hung on the cross. He was nailed there, His hands and feet. It must have been brutal agony. He could have stopped

185

His death at any time but He willingly bore the sins of the world. His
shed blood takes away all sin. What freedom! What amazing love for me!

"I said to myself: belief is everything," said Job.

Lily's dad often said that, and usually after reading about
the atrocities in the world, which made him upset. 'Lily,' he'd
add, 'God's got His hand on the big lever in the sky. One of
these days, He's going to pull it.' Her father pretended to pull a

lever while making a creaking sound. 'Those who didn't repent will go to Hell, but those who did will be forgiven.'

Philip pulled his shoulders back. "Belief *is* everything. So much rides on it."

"Elstar, the anointed of this world of Whule, has the power to wipe a dirty slate clean. He is EL's remedy," said John, beaming.

Elstar descended Circle Rock. The butterflies returned to Briella as he entered a path through rocky walls, walking on top of the snow.

"Footprints! I see his footprints in the snow!" exclaimed Hannah, tapping her horse to follow.

Deborah looked down at the tracks and followed Hannah. "This is so exciting! Let's get going!"

Habakkuk swished his reins. "There is deep snow in the next section. Then, we'll be on the dreaded plateau. Brace yourselves. It will not be pretty."

Queen Esther rode behind Habakkuk. "We have nothing to fear. We follow Elstar, creator of this world and universe. Maintain self-control, everyone. It will all be for our good in the end, even if we die now."

Victormane picked his steps through snow two feet deep in some places. Lily's boots dragged in the snow but worry kept her mind off her cold feet. The howling wind ripped across her face as she let the queen's words circle in her mind. With freezing fingers, she readjusted her scarf where it fell, hoping all would end well soon.

When they came out of the Gosi Pass, the path ended on a barren rocky plateau with no snow. Light from their lanterns dissipated into the dark, smoky sky.

Habakkuk pointed. "This is Sapphira's Wasteland."

Habakkuk was right. The scene was not pretty but Lily didn't think it would be as bad as this! She forced a swallow as she gazed across a barren, brown valley with sharp mountains at the back that pierced through black smoke. Smoky billows poured onto the immense wasteland void of any lush green plant.

Philip rode past her, tapping her on the shoulder. "Come on. It's not as bad as it looks." He took his horse to the edge of the plateau for a better look.

"Yeah," said Paul as he rode past too. "It's worse!" Catching up to Philip, he halted his horse beside him.

Queen Esther patted Lily's arm. "Courage, Lily. Even now, have courage."

Why would Elstar bring us to this?

Lily's head grew dizzy. She wanted to turn Victormane around and run him back through the Gosi Pass. Then she heard a bleat and saw Elstar looking up at her. *He's just a little lamb and yet, so powerful. I will keep trusting him.*

"Elstar must know what he's doing," said Mary.

Lily and her friends dismounted and stood side by side, overlooking Sapphira's Wasteland. Lily peered down the sheer drop off, her heart pounding in her chest from the height. She stepped back a safe distance, still holding Victormane's reins. *I'm sure Victormane knows not to get too close to the edge.*

Habakkuk pointed. "There's the Gambrel."

Four bonfires burned around a small hill. In the light from the fires, a cross with a coat hanger formed the trunk of a dead tree.

"The flames around the Gambrel burn to the north, south, east, and west," said Habakkuk. He pointed to the back border of the wasteland where the range of jagged mountains stretched. "There are the Dreading Mountains. Sapphira's castle lies behind them. Gomorr is there." Habakkuk pointed to a mountain on the left side of the wasteland. Rows of bonfires blazed at the bottom of the mountain and on the perimeter wall of a city perched on top.

To the right of the wasteland, more bonfires burned along the edge of a city wall that stretched before dark buildings under dark skies. Large beasts guarded the gate. "And there is Si." Habakkuk looked to a stone structure further down the plateau where the path had turned to. "And there is the Gosi Post. We've been watching this place for a long time."

A wall of stone surrounded the Gosi Post, a structure larger than the Caper Post. Two launchers towered above with a pile of large rocks beside them ready to be hurled.

Elstar bleated. Lily bent down to hold his head in her hands. "I don't understand. What now?" Elstar rubbed his neck against her hand and then trotted toward the Gosi Post.

"Lean not on your own understanding," said Queen Esther.

Queen Esther's confidence helped Lily to be confident. She tried to match her sure expression.

Elstar passed the Gosi Post and walked down a road.

Where is he going? Should we be following him? In the eerie night air, Lily watched as he went out of sight. She whispered another Bible verse. "Trust in the LORD with all thine heart and lean not onto thine own understanding." She leaned into Victormane's neck.

"Peace, Lily," said Deborah. "Even now, when the end is upon us." Deborah's black-tipped ears sprang forward.

Metal machinery resonated across the foreboding wasteland. Lily clutched Victormane's mane when a horn blasted from the city of Si and the sound carried across the plain beneath them. Her heart pounded when loud clanks ricocheted from Si's large gate being opened. When trolls lumbered out followed by soldiers, their armor clanked as they marched and assembled for war. Lily forced air in and out of her lungs as a chariot emerged out of the city. The robed driver whipped two large oxen. *Are we doomed? I'm sure they can see us up here on this plateau. Will Briella be able to fight a whole army?*

The army finished pouring out of the city of Si. When lines were formed, the robed driver lifted his arm, the horn blasted again, the army grunted together, and then stood still, as quiet as dead mice.

Lily looked away, burying her face into Victormane's neck until the sound of hooves stampeding made her look toward Gomorr.

In the darkness, she strained to see a group of forty or more riders racing toward them. They rode fast, whipping their horses hard and hollering as they approached the plateau. The leader waved a torch and his long glowing red coat flapped in the air behind him. A gold necklace swung from side to side as he drove his charging steed. Men and women dressed in red cloaks lined up beside him, looking up from the wasteland to the plateau.

"I am Ayne!" yelled the leader with the necklace. "I keep the Temple of Gom." His horse wavered backward and then reared up on its two back legs. "Give your allegiance to Sapphira! We will *all* be blessed in the end. I have foreseen it!" His voice carried to the height of the plateau while their horses twitched and neighed. They shook their manes and jolted backward and forward as the riders struggled to hold the line they formed.

Briella's butterflies fluttered furiously. She spouted back, "We give allegiance to no one but Elstar. He comes here to make war!" Her voice soared off the plateau and her white gown shown brilliantly bright.

"We will come up and speak with you. If you listen, the Si army won't attack you," yelled back Ayne. The men and women hissed and laughed.

Lily's stomach turned, seeing a mental image of them reaching them on the plateau.

Until light shimmered before her, melting the image. A bright glow appeared and intensified. It took the shape of an immense head. Lily's mouth dropped open as she leaned forward and gazed at the side profile of a soldier's head, motionless like a statue. The giant soldier, stern and unmoving, stared across Sapphira's Wasteland, the rest of his body out of sight from Lily and her friends standing on top of the plateau.

Mary tugged at Lily's arm. "What do you see, Lily?"

Lily raised her eyebrows. "A giant soldier! Don't you see him?"

Mary strained to see, peering in the night sky until her eyes widened. "Yes! I do! I see him!"

Lily beamed at Mary, glad she could see him.

John stepped back. "I see the angel as well!"

More lights appeared in front of them.

"Nine of them, by jove!" said Job, laughing.

The citizens from Gomorr also saw nine giant angelic soldiers and screamed. They drew swords and waved them in the air on agitated horses. The nine angels drew their swords, the sound of metal leaving sheaths that echoed across Sapphira's Wasteland. Lily plugged her ears. When they held their swords motionless over their heads, she unplugged them. Horses bolted and all the men and women raced back to Gomorr except the leader.

"Surrender to Sapphira! We will *all* be blessed in the end! I have foreseen it!" Ayne could barely control his horse.

An angelic soldier looked down and took a step toward Ayne. The step shook the ground like an earthquake. Ayne yanked his horse and whipped it as hard as he could back to Gomorr. Lily and her friends watched the frantic riders flee with fragments of flinging dust.

Then the army of Si yelled and hollered and forced itself into the gate of their city but quickly, the entrance clogged up. So they ran along the city wall screaming, their armor clanking as they retreated.

The angel stepped back in formation. Then he and the other bright soldiers slowly disappeared.

Briella yelled from the plateau, "Ayne has foreseen nothing! Elstar holds all the keys in the world of Whule. Accept him in your heart before it is too late!"

Lily looked left and right. She and her friends gripped their horses' reins and faced the Gambrel. She took a quivering breath as her chest sputtered. A light disturbed the darkness on the wasteland. It drew her attention. Elstar's glowing fleece shone bright against the barren ground as he walked onto the wasteland and toward the Gambrel hill. Beneath hanging darkness, he climbed the small hill surrounded by four fires, stood in front of the Gambrel tree, and faced the plateau.

Why is Elstar standing there? It's a terrible place for him to be.

Elstar looked from the Gambrel to the plateau. He waited. The sounds of the retreating Si army faded into the distance. He waited until all was silent and a darkness that could be felt settled on the plateau.

A touch on Lily's elbow startled her and she turned to face Finn. He had spoken her name softly and his expression was more serious than she had ever seen. He peered into her eyes. "Do you really think there is a Savior?"

Lily's ears grew warm. She smiled and nodded her head.

"*How* can you be sure?"

Finn's question gnawed at Lily. She repeated it in her mind, wondering what she could say. She remembered how she became saved, led by her mother. They had knelt by the bed and Lily repeated her mother's prayer, fully believing. Then, the only answer she knew came out. There was no doubt in her mind.

"You *can* be sure. Would you like to ask Elstar into your heart?"

Finn kneeled and bowed his head. "Yes."

His answer and posture caught Lily off guard. She was expecting a 'no.' Had he been thinking about this for a while? She scrambled to know what to do next.

"Then … let's pray. Just … repeat after me." Lily bowed her head in front of Finn and closed her eyes. "Dear Lord,"

Finn repeated.

"Thank you for loving me."

Finn echoed her words.

"I'm sorry for my sins."

Finn matched Lily's apology.

"Please forgive me."

Finn claimed the plea his own.

Then Lily spoke to Jesus. "You are my Creator's remedy, my Rock, and my salvation. I give you my heart."

Lily opened her eyes to see Finn with his eyes still closed. He repeated those very words into the night air, clear and true.

When Finn opened his eyes to meet Lily's, his soft gaze drew tears that welled in her eyes. Unable to speak and choked on her happiness, Lily looked around at her friends, hoping they saw what just happened. Their smiles told her that they had. She looked back at Finn and surprised herself when she touched her forehead to his. Then she softly said, "That's all it took."

A warm glow rested on the humble face of Finn.

"Look," whispered Mary, pointing to the Gambrel. "There he is. Elstar."

Chapter Fourteen

Of A Long Skip

Elstar's body grew brighter under the hanging darkness of Sapphira's Wasteland until everyone saw the lamb standing on the Gambrel hill.

Finn's wide-opened mouth let Lily know he could see him too. "I ... I see him!"

Lily beamed at her friends with a twinkle in her eyes as John took a step back with a huge smile on his face. Hannah and Deborah put their hands to their cheeks as their faces lit up, their long ears springing back. Job and Joseph pressed their hands to the tops of their heads and yelled 'yes!' Mary covered her mouth with both hands as Paul, Philip, and Queen Esther dropped to their knees. Briella bowed her head while guards cheered in front of the Gosi Post.

Lily tipped her head back with her arms up in a 'Victory V' and shouted, "Yes!" Her friends could now see Elstar as she saw him!

Elstar grew brighter. Light beams shot from his body and pierced the dark sky. Wind kicked up dust spirals across the wicked wasteland. The ground shook. The vibration traveled up Lily's legs. A low rumble bounced off the Dreading Mountains and echoed back to the plateau. Dark clouds in the sky swirled like someone stirring a big pot of stew. And it kept stirring by itself.

Lily's skin tinged and her eyes dazzled when Elstar's body metamorphosed from a lamb having white curly fleece into a larger animal with a brown hide. He shook a full mane.

Elstar had become a lion!

He opened his large jaw and roared. Lily plugged her ears. Elstar's fierce cry boomed across the entire plain. Goose bumps spread across Lily's back.

Then Elstar stood on his back paws and they morphed into legs. His front paws became arms. In a flash of lightning, Lily gaped as Elstar transformed into a man with lamblike ears!

When Elstar the man smiled at Lily and her friends on the plateau, she smiled back. Then Elstar turned and faced the Dreading Mountains. He raised his arms. A large foreboding castle from behind floated up into the sky. With a swish of his hands, Elstar flung the castle into the current in the sky. A chill ran down Lily's back as thunder echoed down the Dreading Mountains. She ducked as dragons and trolls flew overhead into the swirly sky stew mixture slamming into Sapphira's stone structure.

Shapes from Gomorr darted into the sky as if being sucked up by a vacuum cleaner. Ayne tumbled over Lily's head, his gold necklace flinging from his neck. The horse riders of Gomorr that wore red and were still mounted on their steeds followed behind, unable to turn their horses away from the force drawing them in. Lily covered her mouth as their bodies whipped around as if caught in a tornado. The twister circled high above the wasteland with only a mild wind reaching Lily and her friends on the plateau.

The Si army rocketed up into the suspended twirling mixture. Trolls, soldiers, and citizens with cropped ears whisked over Lily's head.

Lily turned to see others from further out streak across the sky and join the current. She recognized the robed commander from the bottom of Gala Lake, still in a burning boat as the evil men sailed overhead, lake weed hanging from the oars. She saw the priest from the steps of the Temple of the Cropped Ear somersault by. His followers soared behind him, including the young woman with cut ears from the ceremony, still wearing a red gown.

Captain Grouse, sitting at the oars of *Salty,* peered over the edge of the rowboat with a confused look on his face and then catapulted into the swirl.

Then, a large man who clutched something close to his chest flew in. It was Buzz! He still held the blue diamond necklace. He reached out his hand for Lily and shouted something but in the violent wind, Lily couldn't hear what he said. As he was sucked into the tow, tears welled in Lily's eyes.

Elstar rose into the sky and hovered over the Gambrel. Lily gawked at the wasteland turning brick red beneath him. Spouts of fire flamed up between cracks in lava rock. Bubbling out of molten ground, a huge lake of fire boiled. Lily's heart pounded in her ears.

Elstar dropped his arms, and the swirling stew mixture plunged into the lake of fire, flames splashing as high as the peaks of the Dreading Mountains.

Briella placed her hand on Lily's shoulder. Peace and comfort spread through her body as she watched the plunge of the evil citizens. A figure in the center of the lake with a crown of teeth clawed for the sky.

Lily touched Briella's hand.

"Is that Sapphira?" asked Lily.

"Yes," said Briella.

The evil sorceress tried to escape the lake of fire. Panic skewed her distorted face. She screamed as flames licked her face. As she melted into the crackling molten rock, her screams grew weaker until they could be heard no more. The nightmarish scene was more nauseating than anything Lily had ever seen.

Lily let out a sigh when the last of the swirling vortex sunk into boiling lava rock. The lake of fire disappeared into the ground, shrinking, until it completely faded away. Barren ground returned.

Lily looked left and right with her eyes, keeping her head still. No one said a word. She held her breath until a breeze touched her cheek. She turned to see a light slice through the darkness on the horizon. Orange, yellow, pink, and red bands grew in intensity and fanned across the dark sky.

Lily squeezed Briella's hand as a warm gold color below the horizon intensified. Then, the colorful banners dissipated in its penetrating light.

Dawn!

Sunshine poured across a cobalt blue sky. In the rays of the sun, the dead Gambrel tree on the small hill sprouted mature green leaves and white blossoms. Openings appeared in its trunk forming into the shape of a gambrel.

Elstar smiled at Lily and her friends on the plateau. Raising his arms, he said, "Behold! The new Whule has come!"

His clear voice resonated in Lily's ears. She was sure that everyone must have heard it.

Elstar faced the Gambrel tree. "You will be called The Tree of Love Shown. Citizens will remember the love I have for my creation from my sacrifice on the Gambrel."

Lily pressed her hands against her face when grass sprouted on what was the wasteland and quickly spread over the massive barren plain under the blue sky. Yellow daffodils popped up in the new grass as far as the eye could see.

Elstar looked across the plain and gestured to the now blooming field. "This field will be called The Daffodil Field of Joy! There will be joy in this land. Those who followed me in the old Whule will enjoy what I provide in the new Whule!"

Elstar lifted an arm where the wicked city of Si had been. A large crystal lake formed. New buildings arose, many with glass windows catching the sun's rays. "Behold! The City of

Crystal by Peaceful Lake. My citizens will enjoy eternal peace in its dwellings by clear waters leading to even more clear waters!"

Lily smiled, thrilled to hear the joyful inflection in Elstar's voice.

Elstar faced where the Dreading Mountains had been. "From now on, these mountains will be called The Peaks of Patience. From magnificent heights, we will look upon The Tree of Love Shown!"

Elstar turned, and with a wave of his hand, the Gomorr mountain changed into a mountain with a cascading waterfall. "The Waterfall of Kindness will be ever-flowing, reminding everyone of my eternal kindness."

Mary whispered to Lily, her eyes sparkling, "Look! There's a forest forming."

"Behold!" continued Elstar, "The Forest of Great Goodness. In my kingdom, only goodness thrives." He looked at Mary and smiled.

Lily glanced at Mary and they giggled.

A huge mountain emerged behind The Peaks of Patience.

"See beyond! There is Faithful Mountain! We shall climb it together. Much can be seen from its height and we will enjoy its buried treasure."

He pointed down the mountain. "And there, many hours will be spent floating on Gentle Flowing River. Boats will be built to ride on its calm current. See the sparkling jewels lining the river bank reflecting the new day's light? They are The Blue Diamonds of Self-Control. Harvest its bounty. There are more than a kajillion!" He glanced at Lily and her heart fluttered.

"The resources of my kingdom cannot be exhausted. All is made new by my hand!"

John took off his coat and tossed it on a rock. "Amazing! And the weather is perfect!"

Paul shed his coat and hat. "It's like instant summer! Let's go meet Elstar!" He steadied his horse and then mounted.

"Yes, let's!" said Deborah. She, Paul, and everyone shed their coats as well before taking off on their horses.

Philip helped Lily climb onto Victormane's back. A little nervous to meet Elstar the person, Lily gently tapped her horse's sides hoping Victormane would trot slow. But he took off running with the other horses. Lily held tight to the reins and his withers.

When Lily and her friends reached the field, Paul let go of the reins of his running horse, tilted his head back and let his arms fling out as he rode—a picture of pure bliss and trust. Joseph and Philip hollered cheers and Deborah laughed. They too let go of their reins and extended their arms out as their horses ran through the daffodils.

Lily wasn't about to let go but clung to Victormane's mane until they reached the base of the Gambrel hill.

She dismounted, turned, and watched as the horses planted their right hooves in the grass before them and then curled their left hooves beneath their chest. They bowed their heads, their noses touching the ground.

Lily locked eyes with John. He extended his hand to her and she felt her knees wobble. "Now, we meet Elstar."

They climbed the hill together, Lily and her friends, and stood before Elstar beneath The Tree of Love Shown, its trunk carved out in the shape of a gambrel. Lily inhaled the sweet smell of roses filling the air. Elstar's lamblike ears supported a gold crown with many gems in it. He wore kingly clothes of purple and blue with a golden robe that reached to his feet. Behind him, lights fell from the sky that became living beings, some like Briella with short ears while others with lamblike ears. Birds, dragonflies, and bees flew over their heads, and strange creatures with wings bowed their heads.

Elstar stretched out his arms toward Lily and her friends. "I am with you and will dwell with you forever."

Elstar's rich voice resonated in Lily's eardrums with a pleasant tone and frequency.

"Now is realized hope and cherished fellowship." Elstar turned and looked across The Daffodil Field of Joy. "Here come the faithful to inhabit the new Whule. Here come the resurrected dead!"

On the outskirts of the field, people with long ears walked from the City of Crystal by Peaceful Lake. Others came from the opposite direction, where the new sun had risen on the new land. Some walked and some ran.

"Here come the faithful remnant from Jerul, Bethem, and Ephra," Elstar continued. "And places even further away, across generations, and time. What joy to live together in the new world!"

Crowds of people with lamblike ears approached the Gambrel hill from every direction, from over the mountains—walking, running, skipping—all heading toward Elstar.

Elstar faced Lily and her friends. "Greet your loved ones," and to Briella, he said, "And your kind."

Briella bowed and strolled to the beings that had descended from the sky.

John bowed to Elstar. "Your heart is known to me, John, my friend. Now, are those your parents who were once dead but are now risen?" asked Elstar, pointing to them in the crowd.

John turned. "They look younger, and I see an old friend who died years ago!" When Elstar nodded, John's brown eyes twinkled and he ran down the hill to them.

Hannah, who had grown younger and whose gray hair was now brown, embraced Elstar, who embraced her back.

"Go, Hannah. Greet your family," said Elstar.

Hannah ran, Lily guessing for the first time in a long time. Lily smiled when she saw her hug people in her bubbly way.

Deborah bowed deeply before Elstar. "Thank you for eternal peace." When he nodded for her to reunite with her family, she took off running.

Job laughed as he took stock of his now younger features and touched his knee. "My knee! It doesn't hurt anymore! I said to myself, now *this* is the best day of my life! Thank you, Your Majesty!"

"Your faith has healed you, my good man, Job! Go meet your family."

Job laughed as he strolled down the hill to greet family and friends.

As a large family approached from the crowd, Joseph exclaimed, "My brothers! My father!" He thanked Elstar and then Elstar encouraged him to hurry to them.

A man and woman looked up at Mary to which she exclaimed, "I see my parents!"

"I have known them well, Mary. Now, go and greet them."

Mary smiled and bowed to Elstar, then ran to them.

"I am the rewarder of those who sought me. Find those martyred for their faith," said Elstar to Paul, who bowed deeply then put his hand over his heart.

"The martyred are greatly honored in my Realm. Paul, whom you are named after, is there also." Paul beamed, then walked down the hill to his namesake.

Philip and Habakkuk waved to people and, also after thanking Elstar, they soon bolted down the hill. Habakkuk ran beside Philip until he reached a woman and swept her off her feet while Philip happily met people he knew.

Queen Esther approached Elstar and removed her crown from her head and placed it at his feet.

"Blessings to you, Esther," said Elstar as he touched her head. "I have known your heart too. Look. There is someone waiting for you."

Esther strolled down the hill to a man, Lily guessed the former king, Esther's husband.

Finn searched the people. Soon, his features stilled except for tears forming in his eyes. He spoke quietly. "My father and mother." He bowed to Elstar.

"They will be happy to see you, Finn." Elstar touched his arm. "Go. There will be plenty of time to talk later."

Finn couldn't utter a word from being filled with emotion but nodded his head in gratitude.

205

Sunlight reflected on the gems in Elstar's golden crown as Lily stood alone on the hill with him under The Tree of Love Shown. She looked into his eyes and knew they were the same warm brown eyes she had seen in Elstar the lamb.

Elstar picked a white rose from the tree and gave it to Lily.

Lily took the blossom and touched it to her nose, inhaling fully. A gentle breeze swept through the branches of The Tree of Love Shown and brushed the side of her face.

"You have been on a peculiar journey, haven't you, Lily? What have you learned?"

Lily looked down and dug her toe in the grass. She hoped her bad thoughts about Finn and Buzz hadn't been noticed. She regretted that now, especially after seeing Buzz be swept away. "I've learned to follow the way of love although I'm not very good at it."

"But Finn came to his senses, and he became the last one saved in the world of Whule. You had a part in that."

Lily's eyes shined, glad she did that. Then, in a blink, Elstar was gone and Jesus stood before her wearing a white robe. And then it dawned on her. *Jesus. That's why I'm of extreme importance — because He loves me.* She had known this, but a new light shown in her mind as the peace of His presence touched her spirit.

"Trust me."

The beautiful voice of Jesus warmed her ears like a beam of sunshine and His words wrapped comfort around her. Confident that placing her trust in Him was the best thing she could do, she nodded and smiled at Him.

Then, in a flash of the eye, Elstar returned, his lamblike ears supporting a crown and his golden robe flowing in the breeze.

"I know every heart. Those who thought in their heart that I was foolish were cast to the Abyss, as I had written in the Old Text would happen. Those who believed in me remain with me in the Realm, also as I had written would happen. I don't lie, you know."

Lily smiled and nodded.

"It's not in my nature to force anyone to believe in me. My father's law of holiness had to be satisfied in order for anyone to live in the Realm. No one lives here on their own but only by my grace. Without my grace, Buzz was judged for what he was: a liar, a cheat, a thief, and a scoffer. He died in his imperfections, as everyone else did that was cast into the lake of fire."

Lily nodded again, thinking how great it would be to live in Heaven someday where there would be no murderers, thieves, molesters, or sexually immoral people. Sin would be gone. New bodies would somehow be incapable of sinning, all because of the sacrifice of Jesus, the Son of God.

Elstar looked across the mass of people gathering. "I made the way for all here. Those who believed in me gained passage. Those who did not are not here. The way is shut for them. It is a different Whule— one hard to comprehend unless you've been changed in it." He looked at Lily. "You have not been changed yet because this is not your world, but there is a time for you, in your world."

Elstar picked another rose from The Tree of Love Shown and breathed its fragrance. "I love my creation. I proved that by my payment on the Gambrel."

Lily nodded again, knowing Jesus made the highest payment for lost souls.

Elstar touched Lily's shoulder. "Now, you must be hungry." He put his hands to his mouth and called out for all to hear, his voice filling the air as clear as a bell. "Let the Feast of the Nine Fruits begin!"

At the base of the hill, an ornate wooden table sprouted from the ground like a fast-growing tree. Extensions grew around the hill and then nine tables from the circled table stretched across The Daffodil Field of Joy in nine different directions until out of sight. High-back chairs formed at the network of tables. The strange creatures with wings, including Briella, arched their arms for Elstar to walk under. He took Lily by the hand and they descended the hill together.

When Elstar stood at the head of the table, a woman with lamb ears approached him. The woman opened her arms to embrace him. "My son."

"Mother," said Elstar.

Lily watched them hug as vibrant smiles spread across their faces and tears of joy welled in their eyes. Then Lily saw the beaming expression on Mary's face.

John whispered into Lily's ear. "Mary has finally met her namesake."

Elstar pulled out a chair for his mother and then faced the citizens. His eyes danced as he opened his arms and then bowed his crowned head. "I thank EL, my father, for each of you, inhabitants of the new Whule." Then he looked up. "Enjoy the feast being set before you, new citizens of Whule!"

Lily ducked her head when a bird flapped its wings directly over her on his flight to Briella.

"Pity-Petty!" exclaimed Briella. She put a finger out for him to land and brought his face close to hers and kissed him. He cooed as Bluey flapped around him. "I am so glad to see you again! We will keep having fine adventures, my little friend."

Thousands of red cardinals carried green leaves and twigs in their beaks and laid them on the table at each place setting. When the leaves morphed into gold plates and the twigs into silverware, Lily giggled. Canaries flew in with a gold cup in each talon and gently placed them beside the plates. A beverage out of nowhere filled the cups. Blue jays darted from the Forest of Great Goodness and brought salad fixings in baskets.

Large owls soared in from Peaceful Lake with cooked fish, lobster, and prime rib and with precision skill placed the entrees on the plates. People opened sacks that flamingos had brought in and set out bowls of cooked vegetables. Purple parrots placed baskets of bread, butter, and honey gracefully on the table. Hummingbirds flitted forward and back with grapes, raspberries, and blueberries. Baltimore orioles grasped handles of platters that hung beneath them filled with pieces of chocolate cake and orange slices. And indigo buntings dashed to the table with chunks of maple sugar candy.

"What a feast!" said Mary, pulling out her high-back chair.

Lily took a seat between Briella and John. Across from her, Finn pulled out a chair for his mother. He placed a hand on her shoulder, paused, and looked at Lily. "This is my mother, Orline. Mother, this is Lily."

Finn's mother reached across the table to shake Lily's hand. "I am very glad to meet you, my dear."

"And this is my father, Charlie," said Finn, indicating him.

Charlie also extended his hand to Lily and she placed her hand in his. As tears formed in his eyes, he said, "I want to tell you I prayed for Finn. I prayed because I knew how stubborn he is. I prayed that even if it took someone from another world to bring him to his senses, then so be it. And that's what happened. You are the answer to my prayer." Charlie smiled at Elstar before taking his seat.

Lily's eyes grew wide from shock. *I was an answer to prayer?* She caught John's attention on her and she remembered his words—that it was to her glory to overlook an offense. She smiled. She had not been given a picture of what that might look like until now.

Further down the table, Philip drank from a gold cup. "Words cannot express how exceptional this drink is! Listen to me talk. I'm sounding quite grand!"

"The best I've ever had!" said Eth, with restored ears. They laughed and clicked their cups together.

Lily's plate was filled with food. And there weren't any tuna fish sandwiches, although Lily reasoned there could be if one wanted.

When all the people finished eating, the birds came and cleaned up the leftovers. Then, a long-eared man with dark skin sang in a tenor voice as huge eagles flew overhead, Lily guessing the ones from Lambstone Mountain.

Lily peered under the table at the plentiful grass and vibrant daffodils and her heart constricted. Buzz was somewhere down beneath in lava rock, burning. He could have had so much more if he had only believed.

211

Chapter Fifteen

Because of Him

As the tenor sang and birds circled overhead, Lily's thoughts drifted back home. The hot muggy day after school seemed ages ago until she counted the days passed in Whule. Three.

When the man ended the song, Elstar spoke clearly to all. "I have prepared places for all of you. Anyone wishing to live in The City of Crystal by Peaceful Lake may do so. Find beautiful homes to live in. Those who want to design and build their own home may do so. Those who desire to reside in the Peaks of Patience or on Faithful Mountain may go there."

Lily followed his gaze across The Daffodil Field of Joy.

"Kindness Waterfall and the Forest of Great Goodness offer mystical places to live. Gentle Flowing River affords pleasing adventures ending with rich bounty. Walk along the riverbank and find blue diamonds. You may use them for creative works of art. Harness the materials of the new creation I have made for you."

Queen Esther touched her neck. "A blue diamond necklace here will be more magnificent than the one I had."

Hannah pushed her chair under the table. "We will walk along the riverbank together in search of them." Then the chair and the tables began to return to the ground. The absorption of the long network of tables across The Daffodil Field of Joy amazed all who watched it.

"Come with me," said Elstar, walking toward the road to the plateau.

Mary grabbed Lily's arm while encouraging a skip as they followed Elstar.

Elstar called out, "I love stories! I have invested my time in the stories of my created and I will continue to do so!"

Mary said to Lily, "I'm going to collect some of these." She halted the skip and bent down to collect a bouquet of daffodils of which she presented to Elstar. "Do you know my story?"

"I most certainly do!" He smiled at Mary.

As Elstar and the citizens ascended the road, Lily thought about how God knew her story.

When they reached where the Gosi Post had been, a mansion now filled the place surrounded by fruit trees. Elstar faced Habakkuk. "Would you like to live here, my faithful guard?"

Habakkuk bowed. "Thank you, my king. Whule is filled with your knowledge and glory as grass and daffodils cover the field below."

From the view on the plateau, people still dispersed toward The Forest of Great Goodness, the Peaks of Patience, and The City of Crystal by Peaceful Lake.

"And to let you know," continued Elstar to Habakkuk, "I saw Private Wolff and friends walk toward Gentle Flowing River. I'm sure he'll visit you sometime, or you him."

Habakkuk bowed again.

Horses grazed in the field and Lily spotted Victormane. He lifted his head and whinnied to her.

"He'll be happy there," said Philip.

And when Victormane pranced around swishing his tail, Lily knew Philip was right.

Elstar continued to speak to the people. "If anyone wishes to live here, you will find homes waiting for you. Or, you may build your own home into the mountain so you may look upon the new creation."

Elstar faced the Gosi Pass. "We need a new name for this pass. What should it be, Finn?"

Finn's eyes widened. "Whatever you choose, Your Majesty."

"Then let it be called 'Newman's Pass' in honor of Finn Newman, the last person saved in the world of Whule."

Finn radiated. "I am honored. Thank you."

Elstar entered Newman's Pass.

Mary exclaimed, "The snow! It's all gone!" her voice echoed off the rocks.

"Good," said Deborah, with a touch of relief.

Elstar strolled beside her. "No more will any of you endure hardships. But snow can be wonderful. I know some of you enjoy this cold element that I made. Enjoy with skis on trails beneath snow-covered boughs of hemlock and pine. Or enjoy ice. Boots made with blades on the bottom can bring the joy of ice skating down frozen rivers lined with spruce trees.

The tropics are wonderful too. I enjoy many climates or I wouldn't have made them all! In the tropics, a small machine could be built that would enable its rider to soar over the jungle canopy and between varied trees which I wonderfully made. Or let us rest together in hammocks tied to palm trees and look up through, listening to the many calls of colorful birds. Let us count all the different butterflies." He glanced at Briella. "There are many varied places yet to discover as my kingdom has no end."

Lily's eyes brightened and took in all the fresh greenery and blooming flowers along the way where snow had filled only hours before.

"This is how to live," said Elstar, "happy, unafraid, and content. I will keep us all safe and healthy."

It occurred to Lily that even though they had walked across the field, up the road, and half way through Newman Pass, she didn't think she was as tired as she thought she should be.

The sun shone on Finn's face when they reached Circle Rock and he faced Lily. "I will always remember this place. I am thankful to you, Lily. I have new eyes and I breathe so well. I had sensed something here at Circle Rock. I felt a breath on my hand. I thought maybe we didn't evolve… that creation *is* possible."

Lily glowed. "That's good, Finn."

"Then, on the plateau, I *had* to make a decision. You see, I had a sense of urgency, not just because of the evil in the wasteland, but because of my soul. I didn't want to keep going on the path I was on."

Lily knew this was the new Finn speaking. His mortal being was now immortal and his corrupted soul was now incorruptible.

Finn peered into Lily's eyes. "When you figure out what it means to fear lies instead of truth, you end up talking less. I learned the fear of the creator is the beginning of wisdom. When you learn what this means … to fear wrath and fairness, then you fear to tell lies." Finn smiled. "It's a good fear." Then he turned serious again. "I asked myself: 'What is the cost of lies?' If I tell enough, the truth can no longer be seen and I dig into a pit hypnotizing myself to keep going as I go further toward damnation."

Lily quietly listened to Finn's words, aware that he must have strayed far from love.

Finn looked at the blue sky and breathed deep. "And then, I realized my creator's love for me. He met the demand for peace in my soul. I don't know how to explain it except I know he washed my filthy rags clean. He traded places with me on that Gambrel." Finn's eyes watered as he looked into Lily's eyes. "Amazing grace, like that song you sang in the jail. I'm forgiven." Finn regained his composure. "Now, I think I will sail the seas. Or climb Faithful Mountain and look for a homestead." He paused. "I might study in Jerul first, though. I was so wrong! The Old Text is not gibberish. There is so much to learn and so many people to meet. There is a joy I never knew in knowing people! Or maybe I forgot. Things have changed for me, Lily, and for the better."

They walked together to the Caper Post, their friends and many people from the feast. Lily remembered Buzz standing in the window and how he was swept away, then plunged to his fiery death in the lake of fire. *Hell is real—that place of weeping and gnashing of teeth.*

A picture of Lazarus in the Bible came to Lily's mind. He was a poor beggar by a rich man's gate. When both men died, the rich man went to Hell but Lazarus went to Heaven. The rich man begged Lazarus to dip the tip of his finger in water to cool his burning tongue but it wouldn't be possible.

I want to warn people. I want to point them in the right direction so they don't end up like Buzz.

"Are you all right, my dear?" asked Hannah.

Lily nodded.

"You will be going home soon, but before you go, look at that view!" Hannah gracefully swished her arm before her.

Elstar held his hands out from the top of Abar Mountain. "Behold! The sparkling Royal City of Jerul!" His eyes flashed strength and his kingly robe sparkled in the sunshine. Gems on his crown reflected light into Lily's eyes and she gleamed, her mood uplifted.

Light flashed into Joseph's eyes too. "I've never seen Jerul look so magnificent!"

"Nor have I!" said Esther. "I look forward to living in the new city. And see how the blue water of Gala Lake shimmers!"

Finn placed a hand on Job's shoulder. "I am sorry for how I spoke to you on *The Gallant*. Please forgive me."

Job laughed. "All is forgiven, Finn. And the memory is escaping me!"

Finn then turned to Briella. "And to you, Briella. I am sorry for the things I said." He looked at everyone. "I'm sorry to all of you."

Briella smiled. "You are a new person. The old has gone."

As Elstar led the people down Abar Mountain, Job spoke to a man beside him. "Wonderful new creation, isn't it, my friend?"

"I said to myself, indeed," the man replied.

Job said, "Miss Lightfoot, I would like to introduce you to the *actual* Job of the Old Text."

"Hello," said Lily.

"Very honored to meet you," said the actual Job.

Lily, Finn, Briella, Job, and Job and everyone else talked and laughed as they strolled down the mountain together.

Tall evergreen trees filled the woods on either side of the road and the sound of water echoed off tree trunks. Briella walked beside Elstar, Pity-Petty flying from branch to branch while Bluey fluttered above her head as the other butterflies rode on her head and sleeves.

"Enjoy the water from the eternal spring. The water is even better than that of the old Whule. Let us take a sip now," said Elstar. "And if any of you desire to live by Kerith Falls, then do so."

After sipping the refreshing sweet water, the processional continued through the town of Caper under the gleam of sunlight. Lily could hardly believe she was not tired.

Elstar continued. "All towns honor me in my Realm. Love will reside in hearts. Joy will crown heads, and peace will calm minds."

The group of people skipped the country road to Jerul, amazed at their strength and vitality. When they reached the Caper Gate on the back side of the city, Elstar didn't enter but stayed on the road leading the crowd around the perimeter to the front gate.

A white horse met Elstar at the gate. He climbed onto the back of the horse and tied Mary's bouquet of daffodils on the top of the horse's head between its ears with strands of hair from its mane. Then between rows of red roses, Elstar rode through the main gate of the Royal City of Jerul.

Glistening white light reflected off windows in the city. Huge stained-glass windows of a large church with sweeping roofs also reflected light. Across the front of the church was engraved "Truth and Prosperity Forever." The Temple of the Cropped Ears was gone.

Elstar stepped down from the white horse onto a gold-paved road. He spoke on the church steps to the people gathered. "My beloved, Jerul's government is upon my shoulders. There will be no more lawlessness." He smiled at a man and Lily saw that it was the police officer from the old

Whule. When she saw he smiled back, she knew he was pleased.

Lily and her friends and the people followed Elstar into the church. Light from his body flooded the sanctuary and passed through tall stained-glass windows. Pews made of a rich dark wood invited the people to fill them.

"Sit here, Lily, between Philip and I," said Deborah. Lily sat, her eyes fixed on a familiar black object in front. Its glossy top was open, set by a prop stick. It was a concert grand piano.

Elstar faced the people from the front of the church. "Love is the most excellent way in which to live. The old is gone and the new has come. The debt has been satisfied by my shed blood. Citizens of the Realm, enjoy riches forever. Be blessed with friendships and strong spirits." Cheers resounded in the church building.

Elstar gestured to the piano. "Before the rewards, is there anyone here who can play the piano for us?"

Lily smiled, waiting for someone to go up.

Deborah whispered to Lily, "Piano? Is that the instrument you play?"

"Yes," said Lily.

Elstar moved closer to the piano. "Is there no one here who can play?"

Lily froze. She glanced left and right, sure that someone else would play. But when silence fell across the congregation, she caught Elstar's eyes pinned on her. Blood drained from her face.

He looked kindly at her. "What pleasure it would bring to my ears to hear its rich tones fill this church. I know there is one here who can play it."

Lily's heart pounded in her chest. Her legs locked. Had she just turned into a mannequin? It was not possible for her to stand from the pew.

"What if I went up with you?" suggested Deborah.

Briella leaned forward. "And I."

Lily forced a swallow. Deborah tugged at Lily's arm and guided her to the piano while Briella held her hand. Then Deborah and the guardian sat in chairs behind the piano.

Lily ran her hand along the highly polished black ebony concert grand piano which was nine feet long. Trying to ignore nervous feelings in the pit of her stomach, she pulled out the piano bench, sat, lifted the cover, and grinned at the black and white keys. They were the kind she liked, not too sharp-edged but smooth and rounded.

Lily focused on the music she would play, a favorite nocturne she had been practicing. Notes on the written page came into her mind. Taking a deep breath, she positioned her hands over the keys and played the first warm tones.

She played expressively like she was taught—the repeated notes passionately louder. She played loud sections loud, soft sections soft. The bass notes resonated in the piano's long wooden cabinet. The treble notes sang almost effortlessly. In a perfect fit for her hands, the piano played like butter.

When Lily came to the last page of the music in her head where her memory had been sketchy, she concentrated on the tricky fingering section, playing her best. Like a red carpet being rolled out for her, the music came. Notes fell into place. With four solid chords, she concluded the nocturne, keeping her hands on the keys as the sound faded from the piano into the sanctuary, and as the butterflies in her mind took flight and fluttered away.

Elstar smiled. "Exceptional, Lily."

"So that's what a piano sounds like!" said Deborah.

Elstar raised a hand for Eth to come forward. He carried a golden flute on a plush pillow.

"And now, another song with this flute for Briella," said Elstar.

Briella picked up the flute with glee. "Thank you, almighty creator!" She twinkled at Elstar.

Briella placed her lips to the mouthpiece and whimsical notes of the instrument filled the church. She motioned for Lily to play and Lily concentrated on matching harmonic chords as she accompanied Briella. When they finished, Briella smiled at Lily and said, "That was "The Flight of the Butterfly.""

Elstar laughed. "More musical instruments will be mastered. Musicians, artists, poets, writers, builders, cooks, gardeners, adventurers, explorers, teachers, and technicians, to name a few, will enjoy my kingdom."

Chapter Sixteen

Who Loves Me.

A trumpet fanfare signaled the beginning of the rewards ceremony. Lily, Deborah, and Briella returned to their seats.

Elstar stood before the assembly on a raised platform. "There is no need for keeping peaceful relations because they already exist." He faced Esther and her husband. "In the old Whule, you both maintained self-control. For this, you shall be rewarded. In light of this, will you, Esther and Xerxes, be the Administrators of the Banquets of Jerul?"

They beamed. "Yes! Thank you, Your Majesty."

Lily wanted to have better self-control when facing trials.

Elstar walked across the platform and stopped in front of Philip. "Because you were gentle and understood the Old Text so well, I will greatly reward you. Would you accept the job of Teacher in Jerul? There are no false teachers anywhere in the Realm."

Philip stood, his upturned face revealing his pearly white teeth. "I would be honored. Thank you, my Master."

"You might also organize horse-drawn chariot races in Jerul." Elstar raised his eyebrows while smiling at Philip.

Philip laughed. "That has been a dream of mine!"

"I know," said Elstar.

Elstar faced Paul, who stood to his feet. "A new role for you is to be Speaker of Jerul. People from all over the Realm will journey to hear you speak about the events recorded in the Old Text. Traveling extensively by ship will be on your agenda. Your faith has enabled you to receive this reward."

Paul clasped his hands together and bowed. "Thank you for this honor, Your Majesty. I look forward to talking with many people."

Lily wanted to keep the faith like Paul, even around those who had no faith.

Elstar moved to Mary. "Mary, reside in the new Bethem and gain mastery of your artistic skill. Your love for me was shown in acts of goodness to others. You were the first to see me so you will always be honored. When you visit Jerul, you will have a seat at my table."

Mary's lamblike ears sprang up and she curtsied deeply.

Elstar came to the edge of the platform. "Joseph, I know your kind heart. Be in charge of building glass-bottom boats made of silver for the clear waters of Gala Lake to study the fish I have made. Build submarines, which we will design. There's a cavern that leads to other bodies of water. Explore the depths of the Realm, even to the Swishing Seas."

Joseph's face glowed. "Thank you, my Captain." He bowed his head.

Lily bowed too, agreeing in the merits of kindness and goodness, even to the choir member back home who had thrown the paper wad.

"Job," said Elstar, "a younger man! A reward is given to you for your patience through times of long-suffering."

"I am richly blessed on this crowning day," said Job, springing to his feet. "This younger body is already a reward. That old bummed knee is not missed!"

"Good!" said Elstar. "As I know your love of farming, would you oversee the farming community of Ephra? Would you run the Ephra Farmer's Market, letting the land be known for its excellent apple orchards, sweet potatoes, and zucchini?"

"With pleasure," said Job.

"Visitors will come from all over the kingdom to sample fares at the market. Your endurance has benefited you," added Elstar.

Elstar then turned to Deborah as a look of peaceful contentment came on her face. "Deborah, I have looked within your heart and know your passion for the piano which Lily played. Would you like to be the pianist for the Royal City of Jerul?"

Deborah's cheekbones rose with a vibrant smile. "I would."

Elstar continued, "Excel at practicing the piano and become a great pianist and composer, writing scores of unforgettable music."

Deborah bowed her head while shedding a tear. "I'm sorry. I'm not sad. These are tears of joy for you have given me my heart's desire."

Lily felt pleased she had a part in Deborah's love of the piano and knew that Deborah's advocacy for peace was healthy for Lily's mind and soul.

"Hannah," said Elstar, "because you prayed, I will bless you. Share your joy with those who lived in broken bodies in the old Whule. Run with those who never could run but now do. Hug those who could not hug but now can! With new arms, legs, and minds, be happy together on outings. Tour the Realm on bicycles, which are yet to be developed."

Hannah's smile reached her bright eyes. She kneeled on younger legs. "It will be my privilege."

Lily knew she could always pray—anywhere, anytime, anyplace. And spread joy.

"John," said Elstar, "Because of your love, your reward is very great. Would you be the Poet of Whule? Would you write poems bubbling up inside of you and visit with others over a warm drink by the fire?"

John kneeled. "Thank you. I am truly honored."

"I, myself, will visit you often. You always declared 'those who have ears to hear, let them hear' and everyone here does."

Lily heard loud and clear that the best thing to do was to follow the way of love, just like John said.

226

Elstar turned to Finn. "I now know your heart too. Your changed heart has enabled you. Would you be Whule's first pilot?"

A pink flush filled Finn's cheeks. He bowed his head. "Thank you. I don't know what a pilot is but I could learn."

"Pilots fly airplanes. Assorted crafts can be designed and built to soar as the birds and explore the skies of my kingdom."

Elstar addressed the assembly. "Reward is mine to give each of you. The slate has been wiped clean for everyone in my presence and will remain so."

Lily looked down when Elstar had finished. He had not said anything to her.

***

Under a clear, blue sky, a man jumped from a ship onto the dock in the Jerul harbor to welcome Lily and her friends who were dressed like royalty.

Mary turned to Lily as they approached. "How did you get to play the piano so well?"

"I practiced."

Mary chuckled. "You must have practiced a lot!"

Lily smiled and nodded.

"Jonah, are you sailing?" asked Elstar.

"Yes, my Lord, to the huge ocean on the other side of Faithful Mountain. I'm assembling a crew just now."

"Paul knows how to sail," said Elstar.

"Then come along," Jonah welcomed.

"I will," said Paul. "But first, I need to say goodbye to my friend."

"I understand. Later, we'll travel up Abar Mountain, across Newman's Pass to The Daffodil Field of Joy and over Faithful Mountain to the ocean."

Paul put his hand on Finn's shoulder. "This is Finn Newman, the one named for the pass."

"The last person saved, uh? Way cool!"

***

With shorts, red tee shirt, and flip flops back on, Lily stepped out of Briella's cottage and joined her friends waiting on the path. Sadness gripped her heart as she knew this moment would come.

A warm breeze moved the tall blades of grass in the field as they walked toward the circle of oak trees on Lambstone Mountain. The eagles on the tops of the trees flew down, landed, and bowed their heads before Elstar, Lily, and her friends. Lily answered with little bows of her head as they passed the birds on each side of them.

Under the canopy of the oaks and before the altar, Lily faced her friends. "I … I will miss you all."

John patted her shoulder. Rays of sunlight streaked through the branches above. "There is nothing to miss. Let the anointing of the Spirit within you direct your step as you follow the way of love. Love never fails, Lily."

Lily knew John was right from the beginning. Her eyes grew misty. "Love never fails," she repeated, meeting his soft gaze.

Hannah took Lily's hands in hers. "Sorrow doesn't cling to the heart when you trust in the One who is able to lift it. Pray often, my dear."

Holding her tears back, Lily hugged Hannah. "I will. I wish I could go with you, though, and those who were handicapped but are now healed, and tour the Realm on bicycles. I can ride well."

Hannah patted Lily's hand. "Go and ride in your own world, spreading joy. There will come a time for all the faithful to mount up on wings as eagles and to run and not be weary."

Light fell on Deborah's smooth blond hair and black-tipped ears. "A voice like yours is proof there is peace to live by. When you are practicing the piano, I will be practicing too. Use your talent to honor the King."

Lily wished she could help Deborah with the music in Jerul but she knew Deborah was right. "I will."

Job threw his arms around Lily. "Young lady, it's been a privilege to travel with you! As your journey continues, remember that the mighty hand of the Creator helps you face every trial with perseverance."

Lily nodded, wishing at the same time she could visit the world-famous farmer's market. She wiped a tear on the short sleeve of her shirt.

"Now, now … no tears." Job ran his hand over the top of the altar. "Look here. I said to myself, what a fine truth to live by."

Lily rubbed her eyes. "What does it say?"

Elstar waved his hand over the table and the letters reformed into Lily's language.

But the fruit of the Spirit is
love, joy, peace,
patience, kindness, goodness,
faithfulness, gentleness, and self-control:
against such there is no law.
Galatians 5:22-23

"I know this!" said Lily. She looked at the colored gems in the arch of the altar and then at her friends. "You have the same colors as the gems on the altar. Do you represent the traits in this verse?"

Mary nodded happily.

Lily smiled at her and then everyone. "No wonder you've all been so easy to travel with!"

They left the circle of oaks and gathered at the stone markers, Pity-Petty landing on a branch near them.

Joseph said, "Show kindness in the opportunities given to you."

Lily nodded. "I will work on that."

"And goodness," added Mary, holding her index finger up. "Your Creator keeps track of everything! He's good at math, you know. Don't worry. He can help you skip all the way home!"

"In your integrity," stated Paul, "walk one day at a time by faith." He smiled at Mary who smiled back. "Or should I say 'skip'! Long story short, don't let discouragement fill your heart."

"And let your gentle spirit shine," said Philip, sunlight on his orange shirt. "You will be honored for that." Philip hugged her and she hugged him back.

Esther stepped forward. "In all situations, maintain self-control when you walk that path to home. You will reap reward." Esther pointed to the path.

Lily bowed to Esther.

Briella opened her arms, her belled sleeves draping, and pulled Lily close. "Keep your ears tuned to wisdom."

"I will, Briella."

The butterflies flew to Lily's head and arms when they broke their embrace. Lily looked along her arms and said to them, "I wish I could take all of you with me." She looked at Briella. "And you, too. I've never known an angel before."

"Your Creator is with you and is much greater than I. He has already appointed an angel to you, and possibly fluttering creatures as well." Briella grinned with a twinkle in her eye as the butterflies flew back to their places.

Lily hesitated. She looked over her long-eared friends and then back at Briella. "I never found out why you have ears like me."

Briella looked at Elstar and then smiled at Lily. "My ears are as yours to be a comfort for you."

Lily tried to smile but it was difficult. Her chest quivered before her eyes settled on Finn's steady gaze.

"I owe you a lot," said Finn. "Through you, Elstar reached in and grabbed me by my bootstraps." Finn looked at Elstar then cleared his throat before placing his hands on Lily's shoulders. "I will always be grateful to you, Lily."

Lily fought back tears but they came freely.

"Aw, what's this? Tears? There's no reason to be sad. I thought you told me the One inside you goes with you wherever you go?"

Lily wiped her eyes and looked seriously at Finn. "He does."

Finn smiled. "Then trust Him. He can carry you to completion, just like he did me. There's no one more powerful." The upward turn of his mouth and the shine on his face drew them together in a warm embrace.

Elstar lifted his hand to Lily. "Your crowning day is ahead of you. You must return to your world and then your eternal home. It is your world that you must skip through, the one designed for you, and the one in which the Spirit will guide you to the everlasting land."

When he took a step back, the field behind him faded into a white background. With another step, he and Lily's friends slowly blended into the background as the world of Whule faded away like vapor. Pity-Petty jumped off the branch and flew directly into a small, white circular space.

And *swoosh!* All was gone.

The only way to go was through the stone markers. As she walked through them, she faced where Whule had been but it wasn't there anymore—only thick woods. The stone markers vaporized away too. She stood for a long time in that spot, her heartbeat ringing in her ears and her thoughts spinning wild.

The spiraling tune of a veery thrush made her look up. A woodpecker tapped. She glanced around for her bearings. Peaceful Rock was ahead.

Sunlight streamed through lush green leaves over the babbling brook when Lily rested on Peaceful Rock. Time must have passed when a gentle breeze touched her arm. She lifted her head and sat up, hugging her knees to her chest. On the other side of the brook, swaying maple tree branches waved a 'welcome back' to her.

Had the whole journey been a dream? Had she fallen asleep on Peaceful Rock? She had to have been there.

Light reflected on the brook trilling through the rocks and into Lily's eyes. Nothing could convince her more that she was loved by her Creator, and that He would take care of her, imperfect as she was. She would trust Him. She cherished the communion for walking in step with His Holy Spirit, even skipping at times. She knew He was able to help her become more Christ-like each day. He, Creator God, was a vast treasure. There was no reason to be discouraged with hurtful, faithless people. They would ultimately be cast out if they didn't get things right with God. Lily grew a heart for them. She longed to hear 'Well done, my good and faithful servant' from Jesus when she would meet Him, face to face someday. Greatly encouraged, she looked up to Heaven and said to God, "I hear You, Lord."

Lily stood and hopped off Peaceful Rock. She found the coyote path, then balanced herself across the log until, between the trees, she caught sight of the roof of her home. She skirted around briar bushes, pleased with her new-found wisdom. Through the weeds, she walked with a spring in her step. And from there, she continued the long skip home.

I will follow and be welcomed across the water where love dwells and friendship grows, blessed with nine traits to help me face every trial, relying on prayer, clothed and ready to conquer the mountain under dark skies till I reach the end of a long skip because of Him who loves me.

For since the beginning of the world
men have not heard,
nor perceived by the ear,
neither hath the eye seen,
O God, beside thee,
what he hath prepared for him
that waiteth for him.
Isaiah 64:4

THE END

Dear Reader,

Thank you for reading *The Long Skip Home.* I hope you were encouraged to live a life trusting Jesus Christ, the Son of God, who loves us abundantly. Through the power of the indwelling Holy Spirit, we can face trials, even loving enemies.

Other books I have written include *Seasons of Love: Woodland Poems of God's Love* and *Unto Us: A Christmas Poetry Book.* You can find me at poemsandprayer.blogspot.com and on Amazon.

God's true story is exceedingly more fantastic than any fantasy story. May the faith you have keep our Creator's precious promises alive in your heart as you continue your long skip home.

Lisa

Bible Verses to Cherish

In the beginning God created the heaven and the earth. **Genesis 1:1**

For God so loved the world, that he gave his only begotten Son, that whosoever believeth in him should not perish, but have everlasting life. **John 3:16**

But the Comforter, which is the Holy Ghost, whom the Father will send in my name, he shall teach you all things, and bring all things to your remembrance, whatsoever I have said unto you. **John 14:26**

I, John, who also am your brother, and companion in tribulation, and in the kingdom and patience of Jesus Christ, was in the isle that is called Patmos, for the word of God, and for the testimony of Jesus Christ. **Revelation 1:9**

And Hannah prayed, and said, My heart rejoiceth in the LORD, mine horn is exalted in the LORD: my mouth is enlarged over mine enemies; because I rejoice in thy salvation. **1 Samuel 2:1**

And Deborah, a prophetess, the wife of Lapidoth, she judged Israel at that time. And she dwelt under the palm tree of Deborah between Ramah and Bethel in mount Ephraim: and the children of Israel came up to her for judgment. **Judges 4:4-5**

Then Job answered the LORD, and said, I know that thou canst do everything, and that no thought can be withholden from thee. **Job 42:1-2**

And Joseph said unto them, Fear not: for am I in the place of God? But as for you, ye thought evil against me: but God meant it unto good, to bring to pass, as it is this day, to save much people alive. Now therefore fear ye not: I will nourish you, and your little ones. And he comforted them, and spake kindly unto them. **Genesis 50:19-21**

And Mary said, Behold the handmaid of the Lord; be it unto me according to thy word. And the angel departed from her. **Luke 1:38**

Paul, a servant of Jesus Christ, called to be an apostle, separated unto the gospel of God, (which he had promised afore by his prophets in the holy scriptures,) concerning his Son Jesus Christ our Lord, which was made of the seed of David according to the flesh. **Romans 1:1-3**

And Philip said, If thou believest with all thine heart, thou mayest. And he answered and said, I believe that Jesus Christ is the Son of God. And he commanded the chariot to stand still: and they went down both into the water, both Philip and the eunuch; and he baptized him. **Acts 8:37-38**

Then Esther bade them return Mordecai this answer, Go, gather together all the Jews that are present in Shushan, and fast ye for me, and neither eat nor drink three days, night or day: I also and my maidens will fast likewise; and so will I go in unto the king, which is not according to the law: and if I perish, I perish. So Mordecai went his way, and did according to all that Esther had commanded him. **Esther 4:15-17**

PEACEFUL ROCK

I headed for a place I know,
not wanting any clock,
where my burdened ears can hear the flow,
resting well on Peaceful Rock.

By the brook, I'll sit and close my eyes,
where the canopy is thick,
and contentment there I'll realize,
as I hear the water skip.

I will sit for many hours there,
or at least what seems to be,
and I'll hear the water sing His care,
of the love He has for me.

And my troubles will go down the way,
where the ravens tend to flock,
yet the perfect peace of God will stay,
trusting well on Peaceful Rock.

About the Author

A granddaughter of Swedish immigrants
on her father's side and West Virginian roots
on her mother's side, Lisa Belknap made a decision
for Christ at age five. At age seven, she started
piano lessons and still enjoys playing today.
Lisa and her husband, Matthew,
have two beautiful, grown children.
They have owned and operated
a small business for over twenty-four years.
Lisa earned degrees in music and reading
and taught music in public schools for ten years.
She serves as organist and choir director in church.
Because of her Savior, Jesus Christ,
Lisa loves to meditate on His word,
and frolic in the woods.